'I have noth

Zoltan's mouth
rush them,' he c

Penny met his blue eyes and found them quizzical. She said, 'Well, that rules me out, doesn't it?'

'Not,' he said, 'necessarily.' He strolled towards her. 'You need to take a good long look at your feelings, I think.'

Penny swallowed and became aware of her heart racing. 'And what feelings are those?'

'Attraction, excitement . . .'

Dear Reader

Spring is here at last—a time for new beginnings and time, perhaps, finally to start putting all those New Year's resolutions into action! Whatever your plans, don't forget to look out this month for a wonderful selection of romances from the exotic Amazon, Australia, the Americas and enchanting Italy. Our resolution remains, as always, to bring you the best in romance from around the world!

The Editor

Born in London, **Sophie Weston** is a traveller by nature who started writing when she was five. She wrote her first romance recovering from illness, thinking her travelling was over. She was wrong, but she enjoyed it so much that she has carried on. These days she lives in the heart of the city with two demanding cats and a cherry tree—and travels the world looking for settings for her stories.

THE WEDDING EFFECT

BY

SOPHIE WESTON

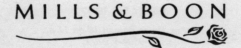

MILLS & BOON LIMITED
ETON HOUSE, 18-24 PARADISE ROAD
RICHMOND, SURREY TW9 1SR

MILLS & BOON and the Rose Device
are trademarks of the publisher.

First published in Great Britain 1995
by Mills & Boon Limited

© Sophie Weston 1995

Australian copyright 1995   Philippine copyright 1995
This edition 1995

ISBN 0 263 78932 2

Set in Times Roman 10 on 11 pt.
01-9504-57270 C

Made and printed in Great Britain

CHAPTER ONE

IT WAS raining hard as Penny Dane sprinted across the tarmac to the double doors marked 'Hospital Administration'. She could feel the rain dripping off the feathery curls that had escaped from under her headscarf. They ran unpleasantly down her neck as she ran down the corridor.

Another breathless day, she thought ruefully. Another day of trying to do sixteen hours' work in eight, of making a thousand pounds do the work of double that figure. Another day when she would have no time to paint. *Again*.

The telephones were already ringing in her office. She picked up the nearest, shrugging one arm out of her wet anorak as she did so.

'St Anne's Hospital Administration.'

'Mrs Dane?'

It was Karen Harris, secretary to the hospital's most irascible consultant. Penny knew from experience that this would be a string of complaints. Too lengthy to deal with yet, she decided, so she said briskly, 'I'll have to call you back, Karen. The other phone is going.'

She broke the call and picked up the next line.

'St Anne's...'

This time it was a fellow administrator in another hospital in the district. She noted his problem and promised to call him back too. He did not want to spend any longer on the phone than she did.

'Last one,' she said to herself, easing the other arm out of her anorak. It fell squashily on to her chair and a strong aroma of damp mackintosh arose.

5

Penny wrinkled her nose. 'St Anne——'

'Penny. Darling, at last. That beastly phone has been ringing for *hours*.'

For thirty years the throaty voice had brought strong men out in a cold sweat all round the world. It had the same effect on Penny, though for different reasons. She braced herself for resistance.

'Hello, Mother! Nice to hear you. But unexpected.'

'Don't tell me I shouldn't ring you at work,' said Laura Brinkman, a laugh in the world-famous voice.

Even down the telephone on a wet Monday, when the audience was no one any more interesting than her eldest daughter, the charm was palpable, Penny thought despairingly. It was only too easy to see how Laura Brinkman had got her own way all her life. And her daughter was no more immune to the charm than anyone else. 'I've tried and tried to get you at home and all I get is your horrible answering-machine.'

'You could leave a message,' Penny pointed out. 'That's the object of the thing.'

Laura dismissed the suggestion. 'You know I hate them. Besides, I want to talk to you, darling.'

Penny's heart sank further, her suspicions confirmed. That meant her mother wanted her to do something and didn't want to run the risk of being refused. If she had left a message on the answering-machine then Penny would have had time to marshal her defences.

'I'm terribly busy, Mother,' she said warningly.

Laura laughed. 'I'd gathered that, darling. We never seem to see you these days.'

It was not a new complaint. What was more, if she could ever bring herself to admit it, Laura knew why.

Laura, an eternal optimist, lived in a world of constant sunshine where everyone loved everyone else, her daughters were beautiful, and their husbands adored them. It was not just that her mother never referred to bad experiences, Penny thought, it was that she did not allow them to have happened. Whenever anything bad happened to anyone she loved, Laura Brinkman rewrote history—gaily and thoroughly.

Penny loved her mother, but too much time spent in her sweetly scatty company made her feel that she would never get in touch with the real world again. Normally she did not brood too much on her past. But after a long weekend in Shropshire she would find herself driving back to London grimly reciting the events of the dreadful course of her marriage in case she started to live in Laura's fantasy universe as well. It made family reunions a strain.

And that, of course, was what Laura would want. Her youngest daughter was getting married and in Laura's dramatic hands the wedding was turning into a production of royal proportions. In the frenzy of happy activity, Laura would want all her daughters about her. In particular what she would want, Penny was fairly sure, was something between a jobbing gardener and an international personal assistant. A conveniently unattached eldest daughter without pressing domestic duties, however, would do.

'Mother, I'm up to my ears here. I can't take any time off.'

'The hospital will understand,' Laura assured her with the happy conviction of someone whose only office work, back in her glamorous teens, had been fitted round kindly friends of the family saying that of *course* she must go to Ascot if she had been invited. 'Tell them your mother needs you.'

Penny considered screaming, thought better of it, and shut her eyes. She took a long calming breath and reminded herself that it did no good to reason with Laura. Stay pleasant, stay firm and don't get pulled into an argument, she adjured herself.

'Celia's wedding—Celia helps you,' she said firmly.

The trouble was Celia, a model with gorgeous eyes and skin and the sweetest of temperaments, could not be trusted to find a shop without losing herself. Organising a society wedding, even her own, was way out of her reach.

'Celia's going to Jamaica,' said Laura, not without relief, Penny thought. 'On a shoot. She couldn't help me even if she wanted to.'

So it *was* the wedding arrangements. Laura wanted help and didn't see any reason why her eldest daughter shouldn't provide it. Penny winced.

The light on her telephone began to blink again.

'What exactly is it that you want, Mother? I'm on my own and there's someone else queuing on the line,' Penny said. 'Make it quick.'

Laura recognised the urgency of true feeling when she heard it. 'I need you home the week before the wedding,' she said with a briskness worthy of Penny herself. 'Things are piling up and I'll be on my own. Your father,' she added in a neutral tone, 'won't be back till the night before.'

There was a range of complicated messages there. Penny did not want to think about them at the moment.

The door opened and Sister Casualty put her head round the door. Penny beckoned her in. Sister Flynn perched on the corner of a desk and began to remove her wilting cap.

'Not the whole week,' she said, scanning the wall-chart of absences that she kept pinned on the wall. 'I can manage a long weekend the weekend before, though. We can get a lot done in four days,' she added bracingly.

It was even true. In the last five painful years she had acquired a practical efficiency that she would never have believed possible in her dreamy teens, Penny thought with amusement.

Laura said suddenly, 'Darling, is this wedding difficult for you?'

Penny flinched. But she said steadily enough, 'Only where it hits my diary.'

'I know it must *remind* you,' Laura said.

Penny's fingers were hovering over the control buttons of the telephone. 'Mother, I've *got* to go,' she said desperately.

'Just one other thing, darling.' Laura sounded distracted. But that could, thought Penny as she listened in gathering wrath, be a guilty conscience. 'Michael's old tutor. He'll be arriving on the Friday some time. Of course the girls and I will all be out with Celia and the bridesmaids and dear Michael will still be in London. So you'll have to collect the professor and look after him. Well, I mustn't keep you, darling. I know how busy you are.'

She rang off. So, by that time, had the other caller.

Penny put the receiver down slowly, tipped her head back and gave a small, ladylike scream.

Sue Flynn grinned. 'Do I detect a mother in action?'

Penny shook her head despairingly. 'See a lot of post-mother trauma in Casualty, Sue?'

She stood up and started to shake out the squashed anorak. Sue got off her desk and took it from her, smoothing it out with practised fingers. She had three rugby-playing sons and she knew about battered clothes.

'See a lot of it everywhere,' she said serenely. 'What does she want? Half your life, by the sound of it.'

Penny took the anorak and hung it on the peg behind the door.

'No, it's not as bad as that, thank God. Though it was once——' She stopped, annoyed at having said so much. She gave herself a little shake and gave a lop-sided grin. 'Don't listen to me, Sue. I just got up too late to finish a sketch and I'm mad with frustration as a result. Mother's not unreasonable. I'm just making a fuss about nothing.'

She ran her hand through the untidy blonde curls, grimacing at the dampness against her neck.

Sue looked at her shrewdly. 'Making a fuss isn't one of your outstanding qualities,' she observed. 'What's wrong? Is it this society wedding?' Sue knew more about Penny than most people.

Penny pulled a face. 'Oh, partly, I think. Partly it's my father. It sounds as if he's not being very co-operative.'

'The wedding effect,' Sue said sagely.

Penny was riffling through the papers in her in-tray. 'The what?'

'The wedding effect,' Sue repeated obligingly. She shook her head. 'They're supposed to such wonderful things. But in my experience all they do is make people fight. They seem to bring everything that's wrong in everyone's life bubbling to the surface.'

Struck, Penny stopped fiddling with the papers and thought about it.

'Contrast, I suppose. The happy couple gets a fairytale. Everyone else has the same old frustrations they're stuck with,' she said drily.

A drip trickled off the end of a curl and splashed on to a letter. Immediately the ink signature began to blur.

'Damn,' said Penny, recoiling. She wrung out a particularly sodden hank of hair and said, 'I know it's too early but I want a coffee. Do you?'

Sue widened her eyes. 'For me it's late, not early. I thought you'd never ask. I'll get it.'

There was a machine at the end of the corridor. By the time Sue came back with two black sugarless coffees, Penny had got her desk in some sort of order, fielded another phone call and switched on her computer. She was looking at her dairy page on the screen. She had still not sat down.

'Tough day?' asked Sue, peering over her shoulder. She passed the plastic cup over carefully.

'Thanks. No worse than usual.' Penny sipped and gave a long sigh of appreciation. 'Thank God for whoever it was who discovered coffee.' She looked at her notepad and pulled a face. 'Correction—it is worse than usual. Karen rang. Mr Perry must be on the warpath again. That man missed his vocation when he became a doctor. He would have made someone a wonderful housekeeper.'

Sue chuckled. 'Being a bit fussy, is he?'

Penny glared at the notepad. 'Some consultants want body-scanners. Mr Perry wants more carpet-sweepers. Last time he summoned me up there he wanted the conference-room curtains washed.'

Sue looked amused. 'Probably just an excuse to get you up to his room alone.'

Penny took that calmly. 'Much more likely he thought I ought to take them home and wash them myself.'

'That's your job?'

Penny was shaken with a laugh. 'The consultants think my job is to keep them happy. And everyone else seems to think that I'm the only person who can deal with Mr Perry—including him. So I'm the target every time he thinks his status isn't being recognised sufficiently.'

'That's because you're not afraid of him,' Sue said. She sipped her coffee and thought about it. 'And you don't go weak at the knees when he smiles at you either.' She looked at her friend thoughtfully. 'As a matter of interest, why don't you? Most of the nursing staff do.'

'You don't,' Penny objected.

'I'm an old married woman with flat feet. You're a green-eyed blonde. Gorgeous, independent, unentangled. Excellent melting knee material. So why do you stay solid as an iceberg? It's against Nature.'

Penny shrugged. 'That must depend on your nature, surely.'

Sue sent her an incredulous look. 'Are you telling me you're a dedicated spinster?'

Penny flushed, looking away.

'I don't believe you,' Sue said positively.

In spite of herself, Penny laughed at her friend's conviction.

'Why not?'

'Well, you married once,' Sue pointed out.

'Maybe that's why,' Penny suggested quietly.

Sue was staring at her as if she had never seen her before. She said slowly, 'When you first came here the hospital grapevine had you paired up with every bachelor in the place. They've given up now, of course. But we've all asked ourselves why. Is she immune? And, if so, why?'

This was getting on to dangerous ground. Penny swirled her coffee round and round in the plastic mug. A strange little smile played around her mouth.

'Why is an old married woman immune?' she countered at last.

'Too many men in my life,' Sue said promptly. 'Too many rugby shirts to wash. Too many cooked breakfasts when I'm out on my feet. I know the price.'

Penny's smile slipped a little. 'Maybe I do too.'

Sue's eyebrows rose. 'Your ex was a protein-heavy rugby player?'

Penny had never tried to hide the fact that she was divorced. She had removed her ring and called herself Ms but there had been no point in changing her name. Too many people knew her by it. Too many people knew about Alan. Not all about Alan, of course. At the thought Penny shuddered involuntarily.

No one at the hospital had ever met him. It was after the maelstrom that she had taken her first job at St Anne's. It had been a deliberate choice to go somewhere completely new, where nobody knew her. Her family had been furious at her giving up her career but she had had to get away from the art college where they knew altogether too much about Alan—where they could guess

far too much about the wretchedness that had been her
marriage.

Now she said carefully, 'Not exactly. But living with
him taught me that marriage and me was not a good
combination.'

Sue's eyebrows stayed up. 'No marriage, mmm? And
no marriage means no man?' She considered Penny, her
kindly eyes shrewd. 'Isn't that a rather old-fashioned
idea?'

Penny kept her cool and met the sharp eyes. She
laughed with gentle mockery. 'Are you telling me you're
the last of the red-hot swingers, Sue?'

Sister Flynn grinned. She had been married for
eighteen years. 'I can dream,' she retorted. 'And you
could do more than dream if you wanted to.'

Penny's amusement died abruptly. 'I don't,' she said
shortly.

Sue was not offended. She swigged her coffee.

'Is that why you're feeling harassed about this
wedding?' she asked, her expression innocent.

Penny stiffened. 'Who says I'm harassed?'

Sue smiled. 'Aren't you?'

'Why should I be?'

'No reason.' Sue crunched up her plastic cup and
lobbed it inaccurately at the wastepaper basket. 'Only
it's another part of the wedding effect,' she said,
watching her friend from under her lashes. 'Friends and
relatives come round and ask, "You next?"'

Penny looked appalled. 'They wouldn't.'

Sue shrugged.

'They *wouldn't*. I mean, it's not as if I'm going to be
a bridesmaid or anything.'

'You know your own family best,' Sue said in a tone
that disclaimed all responsibility.

Penny pushed a harassed hand through her hair. 'Yes,
but—— Do you really think they'd——? I'm not a girl

any more, for heaven's sake. They must have stopped matchmaking for me years ago.'

'Mothers,' said Sue with authority, 'never stop matchmaking until the match is made. And stuck,' she added as an afterthought.

Penny sat down slowly on her chair. She looked, thought Sue in some amusement, as if she had received a body-blow.

'Divorce is no deterrent?' she asked in a hopeless tone.

'Just the reverse.'

'I don't understand.'

'Well, the old guard look on it as a challenge. By the old guard,' Sue explained painstakingly, 'I mean mothers and godmothers and assorted aunts—maybe even the odd grandmother. The old guard like to prove that they can find a better man for you than you did yourself.'

Penny closed her eyes. 'More suitable,' she murmured.

Sue was entertained. 'Exactly. From their point of view there is no reason you shouldn't try again. There may even,' she added wickedly, 'already be a man picked out for you. That's the way they do it in my family, anyway. If he escorts you to the church or sits next to you at dinner then find out if he's married. If he isn't, they plan that he soon will be. To you.'

Penny opened her eyes. 'You're joking.' It sounded like a plea.

'Seen it done,' said Sue cheerfully.

Penny glared at her. 'Do you like spreading gloom and despondency? Is it some sort of revenge on the world for your unsocial hours?'

Sue shook her head, chuckling. 'Only telling the truth—cross my heart,' she said virtuously.

'I wasn't looking forward to this wedding to begin with,' Penny said involuntarily.

Sue raised her eyebrows at this betraying exclamation. But she said nothing and Penny did not notice, too engrossed in her own thoughts to register her friend's look of speculation.

'Now I'll never be able to relax for a moment,' she was saying, half to herself. 'Every man who walks in, I'll be wondering whether he's married.'

Sue laughed aloud. 'That will make a nice change,' she said firmly.

'What?'

'Instead of every man who walks in wondering the same about you.'

'*What*?'

'You just don't see it, do you?' Sue shook her head in mock exasperation. 'It's so damn wasteful. If I didn't like you so much I could scratch your eyes out.'

Penny looked blank.

Sue gave a sigh and said with exaggerated patience, 'There aren't a lot of green-eyed blondes around. Especially not those who look like you do. Men tend to notice. And you don't notice them noticing. It's enough to make you weep.'

Penny looked uncomfortable. 'I—don't want another relationship, Sue. Even if I could. I'm not cut out for it.'

It was obvious that she meant it. There was nothing of mock anger, mock horror in the quiet voice. This was not teasing. This was serious stuff. Sue stared at her, honestly puzzled.

Penny's mouth twisted. 'I know what I'm talking about, Sue. Believe me.' She shook her head suddenly. 'I only hope my mother does,' she added ruefully.

Sue was relieved by this return to her normal tone.

'Well, don't waste your energy fighting her,' she advised. 'Mothers come armour-plated. And they bounce back.'

'But——'

'Ignore your mother. Freeze out the candidate,' she advised briskly. 'After all, she can't handcuff you together. Just look down that aristocratic nose at him and the poor chap will stagger off and drown himself in champagne. Or find himself a spare bridesmaid,' she added with a chuckle.

Penny laughed. If there was a slightly hectic note to the laughter, they both ignored it.

'You should see the bridesmaids,' she said practically. 'They're all models who work with Celia. There isn't one of them who has ever been spare in her life. Anyone who matched up to their specifications wouldn't be available for Mother to make a match with for me.'

Sue clicked her tongue. 'Stop denigrating yourself. I've told you—you're gorgeous. Or you are when your hair isn't in rats' tails and you aren't wearing a smelly anorak,' she added fairly. 'Maybe the candidate likes his ladies intelligent as well as beautiful.'

'I don't care how he likes his ladies,' Penny said firmly. 'I'm not going to be one of them.' She glared at her friend. 'Stop laughing. You're no help at all. In fact, I suspect you made all this up just to come and worry me because you've had a boring night.'

Sue chuckled, not denying it. Penny screwed up her cup and threw it at her.

'Oh, go home and cook some breakfasts and stop keeping honest women from their work.' The phone rang again. She put out a hand to it, grimacing. 'I hope this wedding effect of yours doesn't get any worse. My work schedule won't take it.'

She remembered that exchange ruefully six weeks later. She was sitting on a windy rural station waiting for the last train of the day which would decant Professor Guard. It was raining again, though less hard.

Her work schedule had certainly taken a pounding these last weeks, thought Penny. Since she worked in London her mother saw no reason not to phone her with requests to collect whatever essentials were not available

in Shropshire. As a result Penny had spent an uncomfortable number of the last weeks' lunch hours flying
around the West End on wedding errands.

She had done no painting at all, Penny thought. She
had been too tired, too much involved in her mother's
activities. And too on edge, she admitted to herself now.
Oh, well, it would soon be over.

She looked at her watch. The train was late. That was
standard. It did not even matter as there was no dinner
to rush back for. There was a casserole in the Aga for
when she returned with the professor.

'Darling, throw a stew at the man,' Laura had said
lightly. 'You do wonderful stews.'

'You hate stew,' Penny had said, torn between
amusement and exasperation. Laura had presented her
with the news that she was to meet the man and give
him dinner the moment she walked in through the
studded front door.

'Yes, but he may not,' her mother said reasonably.
She added with a touch of elegant malice, 'These
impoverished academics are usually glad of a square
meal.'

'Even stew,' murmured Penny.

'Darling, don't be touchy,' Laura said. 'Are you going
to change?'

'To cook?' Penny asked sarcastically.

Laura gave the tiniest of shrugs. 'Well, you are going
out to the station.'

'I think the commuters will survive the sight of my
trousers,' Penny said.

Laura had hesitated, then shrugged again. She knew
there was not much point in trying to persuade Penny
to do anything against her will. She contented herself
with a final pointed stare at Penny's shabby trousers as
she and Celia wafted through the kitchen on a cloud of
silk and Arpège on their way to the car.

Penny remembered the look now, and laughed. Her mother had conceded defeat on the matter of her clothes; Penny had conceded defeat over the responsibility for the unknown visitor.

She had tried to get out of meeting him. Her mother had countered her every argument. There were no taxis at this rural station. No one else was available.

'I don't even know what he looks like,' Penny had said in desperation. 'Won't you at least come with me?' she asked her sister. 'You could go on to dinner afterwards.'

Celia looked vaguely surprised. 'Mummy would kill me. She's got this whole evening organised to the second. I've been threatened with horrors if I'm even too long in the bath,' she said with feeling. 'Anyway, there'd be no point. I've never met the chap. No one knows what he looks like except Mike. Use your initiative, Pen.'

'How?' asked Penny gloomily, chopping onions and sniffing hard as she did so.

'Oh, look for someone like Albert Einstein, I expect,' Celia said with a giggle. 'He's a philosopher and *frightfully* eminent. He'll be about ninety.'

So here she was, wrapped up against the evening chill with her fingertips smelling slightly of onion, waiting for an elderly genius and looking forward to a heavy evening keeping him amused. Well, thought Penny wryly, it was better than wandering round the garden, torturing herself with bittersweet memories. Or shouting over the noise at the fashionable restaurant Laura had booked for Celia's last night of freedom.

Freedom, thought Penny with a little superstitious shiver. It was precious. She hoped Celia would never regret its loss. Though Mike was different from Alan, of course. And Celia was older and more sensible than Penny had been ...

Stop it, she told herself. That's behind you now and Alan is dead. Let it rest. Celia will be happy enough.

And if she isn't it's her business. Nothing to do with you. Don't dramatise.

She looked at her watch again and scanned the horizon. Yes, there it was. The train pulled round the curve of track that would bring it to Sanderham. Penny pulled up her jacket collar against the wind and stepped forward.

It was not a busy station but this was the train that brought the few commuters home. Before the train stopped doors were opening and people were jumping out, scurrying for the exit, the car park and their evening meal. It was the start of the weekend, after all.

Penny searched the arrivals for a raincoat and wild grey hair. There were none. She looked again. Even glasses and an air of academic abstraction would have been a help, she thought wryly. None of the descending passengers met that description either.

Einstein he clearly isn't, Penny said to herself, ruefully.

There was nothing for it. She would just have to wait until those with homes to go to had gone and she would pick up the one survivor. Apart from a man in jeans and cowboy boots and another in a railway uniform, any one of the men on the platform could have been a professor of philosophy. She could not guess which of these respectable middle-aged men with briefcases was Michael's old tutor.

She stepped back and propped her shoulder against the station wall. The middle-aged crowd flooded past her. None of them stopped. None of them hesitated. None of them seemed to be expecting to be met. In fact, to a man, they looked tired and harried.

I know how they feel, thought Penny with sympathy. Except the man in cowboy boots. He did not look as if he knew the meaning of the word 'tired'. As he strolled down the platform she saw that he moved with the casual grace of an athlete. Her artist's eye appreciated that classical perfection. He looked as if all his joints and muscles had been oiled to work—lithe and immaculate, at peak performance, Penny thought. Her fingers twitched. If she had had her notebook she would have made one of her lightning sketches.

She gave herself a mental shake. She couldn't hang around on the local station staring at complete strangers, she told herself. Especially at young men. They might not like it and they could get altogether the wrong impression.

But as the stranger came closer she saw that he was not that young. Notwithstanding that air of consummate fitness, there were lines on the handsome face that added several years and a whole world of experience to the picture. Penny found she was staring at him, in spite of herself.

He was very striking. At first sight she had thought his hair was fair. Now she saw that it was pure white. White like the powdered wig of an eighteenth-century rake, she thought, with an odd little shiver. But it did not look powdered at all. It looked soft and springy, as if it would be a delight to run your fingers through. It glinted in the evening sun above a handsome cynical face.

Looking at strongly marked dark brows and the devil-may-care tilt of his head, Penny thought it was an adventurer's face. A face that had seen a lot, done a lot and not cared very much about any of it. Or anyone. And none the less attractive for that.

Compulsively attractive, she realised as one of those dark brows winged up. He had caught her staring at him. For a tiny moment their eyes locked. Penny's throat closed. There was a laughing challenge there that brought all her defence shields crashing into position. Blushing furiously, she turned away.

She ostentatiously scanned the crowd streaming past her. All the time she was conscious of the level, considering gaze as he came closer. Oh, *hell*, she thought, stabbing her hands into her pockets.

Her nerves were suddenly raw with the prospect of embarrassment. He must have thought she was trying to pick him up, she realised. If he approached her then she had no one to blame but herself. She knew she shouldn't have stared. She didn't know why she had done it. She didn't normally.

Penny lifted her chin and looked hard in the opposite direction. The man was still approaching, not hurrying. She swallowed. He wouldn't accost her, she assured herself. People didn't. Not on country railway stations at seven o'clock in the evening.

Think of something else, she told herself. Remember what you're supposed to be doing here, after all. *Concentrate*. With a little start she realised that the platform was almost empty. No one had passed her who appeared remotely uncertain; no one seemed as if they were expecting to be met. It looked as if the professor had missed the train, after all.

Penny sighed, taking her hands out of her pockets. This, she thought, was going to be a nuisance. She might try ringing Mike to find out where the professor had stayed last night but the odds were that Mike was already out on his stag-night party.

That meant she would probably not be able to track the old boy down. She would just have to come back and meet every succeeding train tonight. She could ring the main terminus, she thought, frowning. Maybe they could be persuaded to put up a notice to attract the attention of a foreign visitor changing trains.

'Damn,' she said aloud.

A soft American voice said in her ear, 'Hi, gorgeous, looking for me?'

Penny jumped about a foot in the air and came down breathing hard. Obviously Americans didn't know the conventions prevailing on English country railway stations at seven o'clock in the evening.

She prepared to be glacial.

'I think not.'

'Sure?'

Close to, he was even more attractive. He had a light tan which made his teeth look ice-field-white and his eyes as blue as the Mediterranean on a summer day. In fact they were the bluest eyes she had ever seen, Penny thought. And they were dancing. He did not seem at all put out by her snub. She struggled with a slight feeling of being caught up in a whirlwind.

'Positive,' she said, with more determination than she felt. There was a distinct look of appreciation along with the laughter in those blue eyes.

He shook his head. 'That's a shame.' He looked round the now empty platform. 'Looks like I could use a ride.'

Penny stared at him in outrage. 'What are you suggesting?'

Those worldly eyes were mocking. 'Only a ride, honey, I promise. Unless you——?'

The unfinished question brought deeper colour to her cheeks. It didn't make it any easier to bear that she had invited this insolence by staring at him in the first place.

She said coldly, 'I am afraid I am waiting for someone.'

The dark brows rose and the mouth tilted. It was, Penny saw with a little shudder, a beautiful mouth with a sensual sculpted line that one day she was going to have to draw. From memory, she told herself firmly.

'Waiting for someone? Not me?' he said softly.

'You——' She bit it off before she said something she would regret. 'Definitely not you. Someone old and re-spectable,' she said with bite. 'Whom I seem to have missed. I must go and see if I can ring my future brother-in-law,' she added, half to herself.

She turned a definite shoulder on him. Yet again he was not disconcerted. He put out a hand and turned her back, quite calmly and with great ease. Penny was speechless.

'Miss Brinkman.'

She stared at him blankly. He had a lazy smile that somehow made him look more raffish than even the jeans and the boots did. The hint of mockery was still there but he had cut down on the blatant appreciation, she saw. A horrible suspicion held her rigid.

'I knew you must be,' he said with a satisfaction which made her wince as if he had insulted her. His hand fell from her shoulder and was held out imperatively. 'Guard. Zoltan Guard.'

Even his hand was beautiful—long-fingered and beautifully kept. It wasn't fair, Penny thought. She felt a great wave of embarrassment close over her head. First she had stared at him openly, virtually inviting him to chat her up. Then she had snubbed him—admittedly not with notable success. Now he was claiming to be the honoured visitor. Cool, competent Penny Dane had never felt so thoroughly flustered in her life.

Penny blinked. 'Professor Guard?' she said weakly.

It couldn't be true. Please God, don't let it be true.

The blue eyes were amused but without compassion. 'That's me.'

It *was* true. He found her hand and shook it purposefully.

His handshake was firm. To her relief he did not hold on to her hand. He would have been quite justified, Penny allowed, after her treating him as if he was trying to pick her up. But he did not.

She curbed her gratitude. This was not a chivalrous refusal to take advantage, she thought, meeting his mocking expression head-on. This was lack of interest. As soon as he let her go Penny eased her crushed fingers, rubbing them with her gloved left hand as the blood returned.

Professor Guard, she found, was looking at her with amused comprehension.

'Not what you'd been led to expect?'

Penny strove for self-possession and achieved it. Years of iron self-control gave you some advantages, she thought grimly.

'Not quite,' she allowed. She was getting her second wind. She gave him a careful smile, not meeting his eyes by means of the useful tactic of fixing her eyes on those black eyebrows. 'I'll have to have a word with my new brother-in-law about the accuracy of his briefing.'

Now the decisive brows rose.

'Mike's briefing is all right. He described you to a whisker,' the unexpected Professor Guard said softly.

Once again Penny thought she detected a touch of tolerant scorn. Of course to a dashing creature like this her serviceable navy-blue trousers and jacket would look very dull. Especially as the trousers still bore smudges of flour from the dusting she had given the meat in the casserole. She stiffened.

To her surprise, she saw him note it. His evident amusement grew.

'I recognised you, didn't I?' he added blandly.

'Just as well,' Penny said with a suggestion of a snap. She looked up the deserted platform. 'Did you leave your luggage in the waiting-room?'

He patted the soft sports bag slung over one shoulder. 'My luggage.'

'Oh,' said Penny.

She wondered briefly if the squashy bag could possibly contain a suit. And—if it didn't—what he would wear to the wedding. And what her mother would say. Her mouth twitched at the thought. Suddenly she felt a lot more cheerful.

'Well, that's easy,' she said, pulling herself together. 'The car's in the car park. Let's go.'

It was her own elderly runabout. She had meant to tidy the interior. In the end she had not had the time. In contrast with the clean, unencumbered lines of the man it suddenly looked like a travelling dustbin. Penny started to apologise for the state of the car and stopped herself. Professor Guard seemed to have an unrivalled ability to get her on the raw, she thought wryly.

He did not comment, merely holding out his hand for the car keys.

Slightly to her own surprise Penny found herself handing them over. But a protest was called for.

'Don't like being driven by a woman, Professor Guard?' she asked sweetly.

He looked at her through narrowed eyes for a moment. Then he flung back his head and laughed.

'Honey, you've got some weird ideas about me,' he told her. He stacked his bag competently in the untidy boot and went round to the driver's door. Unlocking it, he opened it with a flourish and stood back.

Penny felt herself flushing. Wrong-footed again!

'Thank you,' she said arctically, getting in.

He grinned down at her and dropped the keys into her lap before closing the door on her.

'You obviously think I'm a hobo. But I was brought up to be a gentleman,' he drawled.

He went round to the passenger side before she could answer and swung lithely into the car. Penny looked away. She had been right about the muscles—he was an ultra-fit hobo.

She set the car in motion, conscious of him watching her. It took a special effort not to fumble the controls. Now, why? she thought, annoyed.

As they swung out of the car park her companion stretched his long legs in front of him and pushed back his seat as far as it would go.

'Tell me,' he drawled. 'What were you expecting?'

Penny sent him a quick, assessing look from under her lashes and decided to tell him the truth. Maybe that would shake that impossible cool, she thought balefully.

'Albert Einstein,' she told him with satisfaction.

There was a blank silence.

'Einstein?'

'That's what they told me to look for. I was expecting someone vague and elderly and brilliant,' Penny said crisply. 'Possibly with a violin.'

His shoulders began to shake.

'Einstein,' he said again. He seemed delighted. 'If Mike told you that, you're right; his briefing does need some improvement.'

'To be honest, I don't know what Michael said,' Penny admitted. 'I got your description second-hand. From my sister Celia, along with the time of your train.'

'It was good of you to meet me anyhow,' Zoltan Guard said easily. 'And to put me up. I expected to be sleeping on Mike's floor.'

Penny restrained herself from saying that from the look of him he would probably have been more comfortable doing just that. Her mother was not going to take kindly to jeans and cowboy boots at her Victorian-style wedding. But he would find that out soon enough, Penny thought. She did not think her mother's disapproval was going to be much of a problem for him so there was no point in warning him.

Instead she said politely, 'There's rather a houseful, I'm afraid. Family, bridesmaids and so on.'

'Interesting,' he said lazily.

But when she took him into the comfortable farm-house kitchen where the family habitually congregated the emptiness of the house was evident. He stopped and one of those satanic eyebrows rose.

'Houseful? Seems like we're all alone.'

For no reason that she could think of Penny blushed again. She had blushed more in the last hour than she had in the whole of the previous five years, she thought in annoyance.

She said, with an effort at indifference, 'The others have gone out. It's a sort of tradition. Friends of the bride and groom take them out separately the night before they get married.'

He grinned, a lop-sided flash of perfect teeth. 'I've heard of it. Sounds kind of a dangerous tradition to me.'

It was so much what she thought herself that, in spite of herself, Penny gave a small laugh. 'It can be. I don't think Celia or Michael are intending to do anything very riotous, though.'

'Oh, intentions.' Zoltan Guard shrugged. 'Intentions are rarely dangerous, in my experience. It's the outcome you have to worry about.' He surveyed her across the scrubbed ash table. 'Is that why you stayed behind? You're the emergency recovery officer if things go wrong?'

Penny laughed again, more easily this time.

'Not me. I didn't go along because no matter how unriotous the party is it will be too big and noisy for me. My family know that I don't like parties.'

'Interesting,' he said again.

He sat on the corner of the table, swinging one booted foot. He was looking at her as if she were some new species of wildlife, Penny thought, with a return of her former irritation.

'Not particularly,' she said with a shrug. 'Lots of people don't like parties.'

'Oh, sure. But they don't get dumped by their affectionate families because of it.'

'They didn't dump me...'

'Leaving you to meet Albert Einstein while they go out on the town? That's not dumping you?' he queried softly. His eyes were oddly watchful.

Penny's brows knitted in puzzlement.

'That's got nothing to do with it. It was just sensible as I wasn't going with them anyway.'

'Are you telling me you offered?'

Penny opened her mouth to say that she had. But something about the look in the cool blue eyes—or her own innate honesty—stopped her.

'Thought not,' said odious Professor Guard. He crossed one long denim-clad leg over the other and smiled at her lazily. 'Bit of a Cinderella, aren't you, Miss Brinkman?'

'I am not,' said Penny with emphasis, 'a Cinderella. Or anything similarly wimpish. I am a working woman. I go where I please and do what I want.'

The detestable man was laughing openly.

'Excellent,' he drawled. He stood up in a leisurely fashion and came round the table to her.

'And my name is not Brinkman,' she went on, unheeding. 'It's Dane.'

He stopped. 'Married?'

Damn him, he sounded incredulous. Penny would have given anything to say yes. But he would find out the truth soon enough, even if she did.

'Divorced,' she spat, hating him.

He resumed his stroll towards her. 'Surprise me,' he murmured.

'You are the rudest man I've ever met,' Penny told him, outraged.

That gave him pause. 'Am I? You must have led a very sheltered life.'

She glared. 'I'm administrator of a substantial London hospital. Believe me, that's not a sheltered life.'

'One wouldn't have thought so,' he agreed. 'So how come you've never met anyone as rude as I am?' He sounded genuinely puzzled. 'Do you frighten off all the candidates?'

The tranquil tone did not disguise the fact that this was another attempt to put her down, Penny thought. She tilted her chin. He might be a guest in her mother's house but he was not going to browbeat her into accepting implied insults without fighting her corner. She had learned to stand up for herself in the last five years. And, in the last analysis, she had learned to discard the ladylike behaviour her mother prized so much as well.

'Candidates for what?' Penny said contemptuously.

The blue eyes glinted as if he had scored an unexpected victory.

'This,' said Professor Zoltan Guard quite gently.

CHAPTER TWO

IT WAS not a passionate kiss. Over the distance of years Penny remembered passion with shuddering clarity. This had nothing in common with what she remembered.

Instead it was a slow, reflective exploration of her lips. It felt as if he was kissing her to see if he liked the taste, Penny realised.

It was a disconcerting thought, and not an altogether flattering one. She flinched in his arms.

'What are you *doing*?' she said in muffled protest.

The arms were strong. Well, she might have guessed that from the ease with which he had detained her on the platform. Penny, knowing far too much about the physical strength with which a man could overwhelm a woman, went very still.

He did not release her. But the unpredictable guest raised his head and looked at her. Meeting the blue eyes, Penny realised with indignation that he was enjoying himself hugely.

'It's called kissing,' he said helpfully.

Penny let out a little breath of exasperation. To her relief, though she did not let him see it, the incipient panic began to subside.

'I know what it's called,' she retorted.

She put her arm across his chest and pushed hard to lever herself away from him. She was fit and was used to thinking herself strong for a woman. If she had been this fit when Alan——

She broke off the thought. With a slight shock she realised that, fit or not, she was making not the slightest impression on him. He was laughing down at her.

30

'Surprising,' he observed.

Penny's eyes narrowed. She stared up into the amused, determined face and read a challenge.

'What's surprising?' she demanded suspiciously.

'That you know what it's called when you so manifestly don't know how to do it.'

Penny glared at him and shook back her hair out of her eyes.

'Maybe I just don't want to do it,' she pointed out. 'Not just at the moment. And maybe—who knows?—not with you.' The arm was like a steel bar across her shoulderblades. She flicked an ostentatious glance down at the hand grasping her upper arm and pushed against his chest again. With no more success. 'I know what murder's called too,' she added, panting slightly.

The dark brows rose. 'Interesting,' he said for the third time.

This time she did not demand an explanation. She was fairly sure it would be unpalatable and probably insulting.

'Will you let me go, please?' she asked with restraint. 'I would like to breathe again.'

He laughed aloud at that. But the look he gave her was speculative.

'Curiouser and curiouser. Kissing comes in the same category as murder and a man can crush the breath out of you by just putting a friendly arm round your shoulders. Could we have a serious hang-up here?'

There was a little silence. For a moment Penny felt as if he had hit her—one of those frightening, chopping blows she had seen demonstrated in her martial arts classes. Just for a moment she felt as if he had chopped the breath out of her.

She pulled herself together. She was shaking a little. She pushed herself as far back from his chest as she could and tilted her head to meet his mocking eyes full on.

'Don't play psychological games with me,' she said quietly.

The dark brows twitched together. He looked as if he was going to answer but she swept on.

'You're here as a guest at my sister's wedding, not as my psychoanalyst. My hang-ups or the lack of them are none of your business, Professor Guard.'

Just for a moment, unbelievably, his arms seemed to tighten. Penny gasped. All the fear surged up again like a fountain. Eyes dilating, her head went back in protest. But at once he was letting her go.

He stepped away from her. 'Of course they're not,' he said soothingly. He was watching her from under slightly frowning brows. But his voice, when he spoke, was cool. 'I'm sorry if I alarmed you.' He didn't sound sorry at all. Just intrigued.

Penny twitched her shoulders, smoothed her hair and shrugged out of her jacket, ignoring the hint of mockery.

'You did not,' she said with precision, 'alarm me. Do you usually alarm women, Professor Guard?'

He seemed to consider it. 'Only first-year students who haven't bothered with a decent excuse for submitting their papers late,' he said at last, solemnly. 'They're not all women, of course.' He primmed his mouth but she could see that his eyes were laughing again. He put his head on one side and asked blandly, 'Does that make it better or worse?'

Penny put her jacket over the back of a chair and smoothed the shoulders. She eyed him, wary but puzzled.

'Does what make it better or worse?'

'That I terrorise people irrespective of their sex?' he asked solemnly.

Penny knew she was being teased. It was a long time since anyone had teased her. It was annoying but also slightly exhilarating. She could, she knew, give him as good as she got. She smiled at him sweetly.

'You say that as if you enjoy terrorising people, Professor Guard.'

His mouth twitched. 'In a good cause, Miss Brinkman. In a good cause. People have to be shaken up from time to time.'

She heard the private amusement in his voice and did not like it. In a rush she remembered Sue Flynn's theory about unattached men and spare daughters at weddings. She went cold. They couldn't. Could they?

Looking at Professor Zoltan Guard and those wickedly laughing blue eyes, she was not sure.

'And am I a good cause?' she challenged.

His eyes gleamed. 'Good? I don't know. You might be rewarding. I shall have to think about it.'

Her smile became less sweet. 'Don't bother. I don't need shaking up.'

'Ah, but you don't know what you need,' he told her solemnly.

Penny held on to her temper. 'All right. I don't *want* shaking up.'

He was looking at her mouth in a thoughtful way. She became even less sure of her family's innocence in the matter of matchmaking. She was quite sure that Zoltan Guard had never been innocent of any devilment in his life. She pressed her lips together. Seeing it, he smiled.

'Yes, I can see that. It's not the same thing, of course.'

Penny had a sudden image of what he must be like as a teacher—exciting, probably even inspiring and utterly maddening.

'Maybe not,' she said carefully. 'But, either way, you don't need to worry about it, do you? As you're just passing through, I mean.'

Green eyes met blue with an electric clash that almost made Penny retreat a step in pure surprise. Zoltan laughed.

'You may be one hell of an administrator, Miss Brinkman, but I have to tell you that as a psychologist you're nowhere,' he told her softly.

Penny was shaken. Suddenly all desire to challenge him left her.

'Mrs Dane,' she reminded him curtly.

'Of course.' His eyes narrowed, considering her. 'You still use his name,' he mused. 'How does he like having Mrs Dane wandering around when she isn't *his* Mrs Dane any more?'

He was clever, thought Penny, with a little shiver. Alan had hated it. What was his was his forever, he had told her. So she sidestepped the question.

Lifting her chin, she told him, 'My husband is dead.'

That startled him. The mockery fell away like a cloak. He looked shocked. 'I'm sorry.'

Shocked and impossibly sexy, Penny found to her consternation. She averted her eyes and nodded briefly. She was not going to tell him that she had not seen Alan for four years before he finally died in a drunken streetfight in Guayaquil. She was not going to tell Zoltan Guard anything at all.

'You weren't to know,' she said curtly.

He was frowning. 'Mike should have told me.'

She shrugged. 'Why? I thought you were quite satisfied with his briefing.'

Zoltan Guard stared down at her. 'I was wrong. He left out the essentials.'

Penny contemplated demanding an explanation of that. She discarded the idea. She might well not be able to handle any explanation provided by this unpredictable man, she thought wryly.

She said, 'Well, if you've got enough information on my past history then perhaps I can show you your room now,' she said.

He pursed his mouth. 'Enough information for what?'

'Whatever you normally use it for.' A thought occurred to her. She glinted a look up at him every bit as challenging as his own had been. 'Except don't try terrorising me, Professor Guard. It's some time since I was a student but I always handed in my essays on time.'

His eyes swept up and down her in one comprehensive survey—as she would pass a brush of primer over a new canvas. Penny shuddered as if he had touched her. She managed to contain her shocked little gasp. But nothing could prevent her instinctive retreat from him.

His eyes met hers. He smiled slowly. 'Interesting.'

Penny turned away, disturbed. 'I wish you'd stop saying that,' she said, trying to sound irritated. Better to let the man think that he irritated her than to allow him to suspect what that look really did to her pulses. 'It makes me feel like a monkey in a zoo.'

'Monkeys aren't nearly so—intriguing.'

She gave a snort of sudden laughter. 'I'll take that as a compliment. Not every woman would.'

'Not every woman,' said Zoltan Guard imperturbably, 'is more intriguing than a monkey.'

Penny gave up. 'Your room,' she said firmly. 'Come on.' Her responsibilities as hostess suddenly smote her so she added, 'Feel free to rest if you're tired. There's a casserole, but don't feel you have to eat now—or at all if you'd rather not.'

'You're very hospitable.'

There was a dry note in his voice. Penny ignored it. She led the way out of the kitchen and up the dark panelled staircase. 'You're on the top floor, I'm afraid. The first floor is full of bridesmaids.'

He followed her into the low-ceilinged room and dropped his bag on the bed.

'Look out for the beams,' she warned. 'This used to be the servants' quarters when the house was built. They must have been shorter than everyone else. Or they might not have minded decapitating the servants, I suppose.'

'Guess not.' He strolled over to the window and looked across the treetops to the distant hills. 'Fine view. Is that a pool complex I see down there?'

'Yes. My father is mad about fitness.'

'Great,' said the visitor easily. 'I could do with a decent swim. I've had my knees under my chin on airplanes all this week.'

'Oh.' She was taken aback. 'Of course. I'll get the key and take you down . . .'

He flung up a hand.

'Not yet, honey. First things first. You mentioned food.'

Penny smiled at that, her constraint forgotten. 'In the oven. It's only stew, I'm afraid. Warming, but hardly gourmet fare. I hope you don't mind.'

'Honey,' he said with feeling, 'anything that doesn't smell of plastic and taste of rubber is fine by me.'

'Well, it shouldn't do that,' she said, amused. 'Come down when you're ready.'

He did not keep her waiting long. He strolled into the kitchen as she was squatting in front of the range, peering under the lid of the casserole. He was still wearing the ancient jeans but he had changed into a fresh dark blue shirt and a loose jacket. He looked relaxed—and very sophisticated, Penny saw with misgiving. Not quite Laura's academic grateful for a square meal, she thought wryly. She stood up, feeling embarrassed. She wondered how she could ever have taken him for a hobo as he had quite rightly detected.

He stopped, sniffing appreciatively.

'Now that smells like real home-cooking.'

Penny was wry. 'It ought to. It's the only thing I know how to cook.'

Zolton Guard raised an eyebrow. 'So you cook as well, Cinderella.'

Penny felt her temper flicker and curbed it. 'As well as what?' she asked in an even tone.

'Meeting strange men at railway stations while your sisters are out on the town.' There was a note of laughter as well as challenge in the smooth voice.

Penny brought the pot out of the oven and straightened. It was cast-iron, too heavy to slap down on to the kitchen range with all the force of which she was capable. Though she would have liked to.

'I thought we would eat in here,' she said, ignoring his mischievous expression. 'The dining-room is full of wedding paraphernalia. And it's cold,' she added truthfully.

'Yes, I'd forgotten how cold England could be in May,' he agreed. 'It must be twenty years since I was here at this time of year.' He looked around. 'Can I do anything?'

Penny retrieved vegetables from the warm oven. She shook her head.

'It's all done.' She remembered her mother's parting instructions on hospitality and added conscientiously, 'Unless you'd like some wine with it? You could open a bottle.'

'Sure thing.' He did not need to be told where the wine was, she saw. He inspected the wine rack in the corner of the kitchen. 'Something rich and warming on this dark and stormy night?'

Penny shivered, in spite of the warmth of the kitchen.

'Whatever you like.'

He selected a bottle. He did not need to ask for a corkscrew either. He produced a complicated pen-knife from his pocket, identified the corkscrew attachment and opened the bottle with swift competence. He brought it to the table, restoring the knife to the pocket of his shirt.

She ladled casserole on to a warmed plate and handed it across the table to him.

'Help yourself to vegetables.'

'Surely,' he said again.

But he did not sit down until she had served her own food and seated herself. He held her chair for her while she did so.

Penny was a little taken aback. It was a slightly old-fashioned courtesy and she was not used to it from her brothers-in-law. Or from the men she occasionally fed in her studio flat.

'Thank you,' she said, a little flustered. So flustered, in fact, that she gave him her shyest smile.

His eyebrows twitched together. Just for a second or two he stood there beside her, staring down at her as if he were seeing her for the first time. Then he seemed to give a small shrug before taking his own place.

Penny had that odd sensation of breathlessness again. To disguise it—as much from herself as from him—she pushed the dish of vegetables across the table to him.

'Where did you know Michael, Professor Guard? It can't have been at university if you haven't been to England for twenty years.'

'Zoltan,' he corrected.

Penny acknowledged that with a flicker of her lashes.

'Oh, I've been. Just not in the summer. Or what you English like to think of as the summer. I was teaching a couple of terms as a visiting academic when I first met Mike.' He smiled reminiscently. 'They even called me the Visitor. Made me feel like a little green man from Mars. Come to think of it, I guess that's how some of my colleagues did think of me.'

Penny surveyed the handsome face with its hint of wildness, thought of the comfortably sober academics her father liked to bring home for dinner when he wasn't out on the road, and found she wasn't surprised. She took a mouthful of stew, paused.

'So what were you teaching? Philosophy?'

'Philosophy's a big subject,' he said tolerantly. He reached for the bottle. 'Have some wine. You've been out in the wind and the rain too.'

She accepted silently. She found that was the easiest way. You didn't have to drink it, after all. If you said you didn't want any then people would exclaim and make a fuss and try and push you into it. Five years had taught that the easiest thing was to let them fill your glass and then ignore it.

Zoltan poured wine for her and then filled his own glass.

'Logic, mainly.'

She was intrigued. 'Logic? But—do people learn that at university?'

He forked up some food and tasted it. 'This is good stuff, Cinderella. When you get tired of being a down-trodden cook-chauffeuse you could set up a great fast-food joint.'

'Thank you,' she said coolly. 'Do they really go to university to learn logic?'

'Why shouldn't they learn logic at university?'

'Well—it seems so basic.' Penny floundered. 'I mean, we're all logical, aren't we? Isn't that what modern education is all about?'

He waved his fork at her. 'Basic fallacy. It's what education should be all about. We ought to be explaining to the next generation how we reached our own conclusions and how to do it themselves with new data. Instead we teach our kids to memorise facts. They're no better at working things out from first principles than your average medieval monk was.' He thought about it. 'In fact worse.' He took some more food, chewing enjoyably. 'I gave a paper on the subject in Gothenburg last year.'

'Oh,' said Penny, slightly overwhelmed. 'And that's what you taught Michael?'

He shook his head. 'Logic is what I do to earn my crust. My real interest is the philosophy of war. It's not quite a respectable subject—anyway the historians think it belongs to them—so I stick with the traditional stuff to keep the punters happy. But Mike was doing a thesis on the propaganda of conflict. So we did some work together. Have you read it?'

All Penny knew about her intended brother-in-law was that he was some sort of journalist who looked as if he had been brained by a champion every time Celia walked into the room. She shook her head.

'Pity. It's good. You should. Can I have some more of your concoction, Cinderella?'

Penny gave him her sweetest smile. 'Only if you stop calling me Cinderella.'

He chuckled, unabashed. 'Only if you start calling me Zoltan.'

She blushed faintly. It was ridiculous, she told herself, rising and busying herself at the stove to disguise the hint of colour in her cheeks. She was not a child. She had not blushed for years—and certainly not because a man invited her to use his Christian name. Or rather *told* her to use his Christian name, she corrected mentally.

She could feel him watching her. She strove for the indifferent composure with which she usually treated the numerous strangers she found in her parents' house.

She turned back and gave him his replenished plate.

'Zoltan? What nationality is that?' she asked.

'Hungarian.'

She sat down. He took up his fork again and began to eat with expressions of pleasure.

'And?' she prompted.

He looked up. 'And?'

'How come you've got a Hungarian name?' she said patiently. 'Or half a Hungarian name. You can't get more English than Guard, I suppose.'

He chuckled. 'So I gather. It was easier than listening to your compatriots tie their tongues in knots mangling my real name. It's a whole Hungarian name, I'm afraid.'

Penny stared. 'Hungarian? But—you're American, aren't you? You don't *sound* like a Hungarian.' It came out like an accusation, to her embarrassment. She flushed.

The blue eyes twinkled. 'And in Hungary they say I don't *look* like a Hungarian,' he retorted, mimicking her tone. 'The fact remains, however.'

'But—what are you doing in England?'

His look of amusement deepened. 'I was invited,' he reminded her.

Penny realised she was being teased. She glared. He made a face laughing.

'All right. You want the life story,' he said. 'You shall have it.' He picked up his wine and leaned back in his chair, cradling it. 'Born Budapest. A complete mongrel. One Hungarian grandparent, one Russian, one Austrian, one French. Early talent for mathematics. Graduated. Taught. Got bored. Went to Frankfurt to learn computer sciences. Graduated. Taught. Got bored. Went to Cambridge on a research project. Wormed my way into the philosophy school. Thesis. Taught.'

'Got bored,' Penny finished drily.

He sipped his wine. 'Yes, eventually. I have a very low boredom threshold.'

'What did you do when you left Cambridge?'

He looked at her with an odd wariness. 'Mike didn't say?'

It was too good an opportunity to crunch some of that impossible confidence. Penny would have been inhuman to pass it up.

'Mike's never mentioned you.'

He was not noticeably crushed. His mouth tilted in an appreciative smile.

'That's put me in my place,' he murmured.

Penny's eyes sharpened. Too clever indeed.

'It doesn't appear to have,' she pointed out acidly.

One wicked eyebrow flicked up. 'Oh, you like the wounds to show, do you?' He still sounded amused. 'And Mike said you were civilised.' He shook his head mournfully.

Penny regarded him with some dudgeon. 'I think,' she said, 'that I would like to know exactly what my future brother-in-law said about me.'

She met Zoltan's eyes squarely. They were dancing.

'You wouldn't,' he said positively.

Penny stiffened. 'What do you mean?'

'Well, you said you didn't want to be shaken up,' he pointed out in a voice of gentle reason. 'If I gave you a run-down on Mike's briefing you could be seriously shaken up.'

She looked at him in silence for a long time. He looked back. His expression was pleasant but completely unreadable. Then his mouth twitched.

'All right,' she said at last. 'You play poker better than I do.'

'I play poker better than anyone I know,' he said lazily. 'Don't worry about it.'

She sent him a look of deep dislike. The arrogance of the man was truly breathtaking.

'Nothing you could do or say would worry me,' Penny announced.

He pursed his lips. 'I think you underestimate both of us.'

She digested that and decided she didn't like the implications at all.

'I think you've been dealing with students too long, Professor Guard,' she told him. 'You don't terrorise me and you don't worry me.'

He leaned back in his chair and considered her thoughtfully.

'OK. You want to know what Mike said? I'll tell you.'

Penny stirred uneasily. Then sat still. She had invited this, after all. She wished she had realised that she had been inviting that penetrating stare as well.

'He said you were bright. Very bright. And bright enough to hide it—though he didn't know why you wanted to.' He looked at her speculatively. 'I could make a fair guess.'

Penny's chin came up.

'Cowardice,' he said, although she had not asked. 'Sheer blue funk.'

'An informed opinion is always interesting,' she said with heavy irony.

He shrugged. 'Apart from that, he said you were gorgeous though you didn't seem to know it. And untouchable. Well, to be honest the word he used was frosty, but I don't think he can have meant that. Anyway, it's not the right word.'

'Thank you,' said Penny drily.

'No. No. It's only right to be fair.' He slanted a teasing look across the table at her. 'Frosty, you're not. Bad-tempered and combative, yes. Cold, no.'

It was her turn to raise an eyebrow. She was rather proud of the way she managed it.

'You seem to have drawn an awful lot of conclusions about me in such a short time,' she said in a neutral voice. 'I thought academics disapproved of leaping to conclusions.'

His smile—his real smile—she found, crinkled up the corners of his eyes. It was fascinating. She looked quickly away.

'Oh, they do. They do. A lot of real academics don't approve of me either.'

'Either?' she echoed, puzzled.

'Any more than you do,' he pointed out softly. 'It's very sad.'

Penny snorted. 'Much you care about that.'

'Not a lot, in general, I agree. I don't have any terribly British ideas about wanting my opponents to respect me. Though sometimes it can be a nuisance,' he added reflectively.

Penny was bewildered. 'A nuisance? Why? How?'

'When the opponent is a long-legged, green-eyed blonde,' he said deadpan.

It took her a couple of crucial seconds to assimilate. When she did she blushed scarlet. Zoltan watched the colour flood up under the delicate skin with every appearance of appreciation.

'I—you—do you——? How dare you?' she choked.

'Bad-tempered,' he murmured. 'Combative. Not a hint of frost.'

And he leaned forward and touched the back of his hand to her warm cheek.

Penny shot away from him as if his touch were an electric shock. Which in a way it was.

'Don't touch me,' she almost shouted.

He was looking at his hand, shaking his fingers ruefully.

'Wow. Does that often happen?'

'It——' She bit off the insult she was about to hurl at his head. It was uncontrolled, adolescent and it showed how badly rattled she was. She did not want to show Zoltan Guard any such thing. She counted to ten and said dangerously, 'I don't often get mauled by guests in my parents' house, no.'

His eyes twinkled. 'Now, Mike never said you were a fantasist.'

'I——'

'Come on, honey, admit it. Just a hint of exaggeration there?'

She said, 'I do not recall inviting you to touch me.'

He grinned. 'That's the problem, huh? In England men wait for an invitation? Preferably in writing, no doubt.'

Penny was shaking with anger. She reminded herself that he was a guest and that just because he had no manners it was no excuse for letting her own standards drop to the level of the classroom. The primary call room, if she consulted her instincts. She would have liked to throw things.

Instead she said as coolly as she could manage, 'Do you make a career of being rude to complete strangers? Or is it just a hobby?'

He laughed. 'Poor Cinderella,' he said. 'Don't glare daggers at me. I won't tell anyone.'

'Tell them what?' she demanded, in a voice that could have come out of the refrigerator behind him.

'That you're knotted up with frustration.'

Their eyes met again. This time Penny was beyond even trying to disguise the blaze of anger in her own. Her earlier unwelcome suspicion was returning all too vividly.

She was remembering, all too clearly, Sue Flynn's laughing warning. The whole family had taken great pains to make certain that Penny and Penny alone met this man tonight. And stayed alone with him.

'How dare you?' she said, not much above a whisper.

'Don't like the truth?'

Her voice was deadly. 'I don't like people I have never met making assumptions about my sexual feelings and then throwing them in my face on the strength of a couple of hours' acquaintance.'

There was an icy little silence.

Then Zoltan said softly, 'Who said I was talking about sexual frustration?'

It was like a blow in the stomach. Penny gagged.

'Aren't you?' she challenged, recovering, but not quickly enough.

'I wasn't,' he said thoughtfully. 'But since that is clearly what you think—and you should know—I ask myself...' He left it unfinished.

Penny wanted to be anywhere but in the kitchen. She wanted to be with anyone but this man with his worldly, uncaring amusement. She wished it were a hundred years in the future. Or thirty seconds in the past and she could keep her stupid, stupid mouth shut.

None of that was possible, of course. Ignoring the embarrassment was not easy. Nor was the horrid sense that she had dug an elephant trap for herself and jumped right in it. But she was an independent lady who had put her life back together after disasters much worse than an impetuous remark in argument with a stranger. And he would be gone in twenty-four hours.

She swallowed and ignored the slight ringing in her ears. It might, she told herself, even be a good thing in the end. At least it got her determination to avoid involvement out in the open. If her family had concocted some sort of conspiracy to pair her up with Zoltan Guard it was no bad thing to let him know the score, even though she would not have chosen that way of doing it.

She realised suddenly that she had not even considered the possibility that he, too, might be an unwilling victim. Oh, no, she thought. If there was some sort of family conspiracy then this man would be part of it, she was sure. He was not the sort of person that anyone would plot against or involve against his will. Not if they valued their life.

Though it was difficult to see why he would agree. At least it was difficult at first. As soon as she thought about it she could see exactly why he would take it on. He probably looked on it as a challenge. He would find that entertaining, she thought. Keeping boredom away for another couple of days! At my expense, thought Penny, raging with suspicion.

It only needed one confirming detail and she would be sure.

'Are you married?' she demanded harshly into the silence.

The decided eyebrows flew up in comical astonishment. He slanted a wicked look at her. The look said
that the amusement was to be shared. Penny refused to
share it. She stared at him implacably.

The smile died. It was replaced by a slow, interested
consideration which made her shift uncomfortably. But
she was shaking, tense with the need to know. She stuck
to her guns.

'Are you?'

He shrugged, his face closing suddenly. 'No.'

Any unmarried man, Sue Flynn had said. Penny was
so angry she could barely speak. She felt she would choke
with the humiliation. And underneath there was the cold
little sense of betrayal.

How could they? Her mother and Celia—how could
they? They had not even met the man, now she came to
think about it. Just because they wanted a neat pairing
off to tidy up the seating arrangements at the wedding,
she thought bitterly.

She said, 'I think there may be one item on which you
have been misled.'

'More of Mike's faulty briefing?'

She did not smile. 'Probably. I am not in the market
for an affair.'

To her satisfaction, and for the first time since they
had met, Zoltan Guard looked as if she had really startled
him.

He began, 'Mike——' Then comprehension dawned.
Penny saw him realise where she was going. Unforgivably
he looked amused again.

'Mike never told me you were in need of a little masculine appreciation, if that's what you're worried about,'
he told her kindly. 'I worked that one out for myself.'

Yet again he had seized the initiative, throwing her
into confusion. Penny blinked.

'*What*?'

'You don't have to tell me you don't want an affair,' he went on calmly. 'It's written all over you.' He helped himself to more wine and looked her up and down. 'Bad clothes. Bad temper. Left at home to tend the pots because you don't like parties. All the evidence says you're seriously antisocial. Which must be voluntary with looks like yours.' He shrugged. 'Bad self-image, obviously.'

The embarrassment burned up in a heady slow rage.

'So you think what I need is some flattery to give me a better idea of myself?' Penny said with dangerous charm. 'Sorry. Correction: *masculine* flattery.'

Zoltan Guard laughed, the blue eyes gleaming. 'Appreciation was what I said, I think.'

Penny dismissed that with a flick of the fingers.

'What's the difference? I——'

She broke off, startled, as he got up from his chair and came round to her side of the table. He perched on the corner, one long leg swinging, while he looked down at her thoughtfully. He did not touch her. He looked as if he was laughing silently.

'If I said you were a sweet little creature who made my heart beat faster, that would be flattery,' he explained helpfully. 'If I say that you've got skin a man wants to touch and green eyes he could drown in, that's appreciation.'

The green eyes in question sparkled militantly. 'It's also nonsense,' Penny told him roundly.

He shook his head in rebuke. 'It must be a long time since you let anyone get within stroking distance.'

Her heart jumped. 'Mike *did* say something,' she accused.

'No. All my own observation, I assure you.' He looked down at her thoughtfully. 'But everything you say confirms it. No men in your life, mmm? And, I suppose, Mike and Celia disapprove?'

'My whole family thinks they can run my life better than I can,' Penny said drily. She looked him up and down in a very fair imitation of the way he had inspected her. 'And they've got another recruit by the looks of it.'

He laughed, flinging up his hand in a dueller's gesture of surrender.

'Not me. I don't want to run your life, honey. I don't want to run anyone's life.'

Her eyes gleamed. Quickly she veiled them.

'So you *don't* want to drown in my eyes, after all, Professor Guard?' she taunted softly.

She had underestimated her opponent. He gave a chuckle. 'Temporarily, yes. Permanently, no. I'm not into permanence.'

'Surprise me,' Penny said acidly.

His eyes flickered. 'And as you said to me earlier, what is it to do with you? As I'm only passing through, I mean?'

Penny stood up and looked down at him. All her anger, her disappointment and the hurt at her family's betrayal suddenly boiled up.

'I don't like you, Professor Guard. I don't like you. I don't trust you. I advise you not to rely on whatever my future brother-in-law said about me. He knows as little about me as you do. I will, however, tell you two things about me which you may find worth remembering. One is that I don't play games. The other is that if you try and "shake me up", as you call it, I shall make you sorry you ever laid eyes on me.'

CHAPTER THREE

THERE was a long, crackling silence. Zoltan's eyes never left her face. At last he pursed his lips in a soundless whistle.

'You don't beat about the bush, do you?' he said.

Penny pushed her hair back. She met his eyes unflinchingly.

'All right,' he said. 'You don't play games, you don't like me and you don't want an affair. What,' he added mildly, 'makes you think there is any danger of it?'

'I don't,' she said at once.

He shook his head. 'I don't buy that. Since you feel the need to warn me so comprehensively you must have at least some feeling that an affair is on the cards. Rather a brief one, as I leave tomorrow,' he added, that hateful laugh in his voice again. He put his head on one side and thought about it. 'Because I kissed you?' he hazarded.

She flushed. Her eyes fell. 'It didn't help,' she said stiffly.

'So, kissing you is a contributory but not a sufficient cause to put you on the defensive,' he mused.

She looked up. She was dismayed to see that his eyes were amused—and more than amused. There was also a distinctly speculative light in them. Her spine stiffened.

'If you tell me I'm interesting again, I shall throw the stew pot at your head,' Penny said dangerously.

At that he laughed out loud. He flung up his hands, both of them this time, high above his head like a cornered cowboy.

'You're boring. You're boring,' he said swiftly. 'I've never met a more boring woman in my life. Honestly.'

Penny surveyed him. 'Tell that to my mother,' she said drily.

Zoltan blinked. The heavy brows flew up. As he failed to answer she stood up and went back to the Aga. She picked up the heavy pot.

'I will,' he said hastily. 'Any time. "Mrs Brinkman," I will say, "you have a boring daughter."'

Penny put the pot down again, not without some relief. Even with its contents considerably diminished it was too heavy to hold for long.

'Lovely,' Zoltan added mischievously, 'but boring.'

Penny flung him an exasperated look.

'It's true, you know,' he told her conversationally.

He lowered his arms and crossed them over his chest. He was still perched on the corner of the kitchen table. He swung one booted foot negligently as he subjected her to a leisurely scrutiny.

'What is?' Penny demanded, suspicious of that silent inspection.

'You're quite lovely. Even,' he allowed with a grin, 'when you're spitting mad.'

'Thank you.'

He shook his head, his mouth tilted in a wry expression. 'And you don't believe a word of it.'

'I believe you,' said Penny coolly—and untruthfully. She just could not bear the odious patient tone in his voice. As if he knew everything in the world there was to know and she were just a child. That would stop him dead in his superior tracks, she thought.

He looked taken aback. *Good*, she thought. She realised, of course, that there could have been no better proof of the childishness of her reactions. She did not care. She set her teeth and made it worse.

'I'm an artist,' she said hardily. 'I've got a mirror. Of course I know I'm lovely.'

Somewhere inside, her wiser self was looking on in blank amazement. Penny had not behaved like this since she was a carefree art student, still experimenting, still hopeful. It was exhilarating.

Zoltan flicked up one eyebrow. His eyes were bright with laughter.

'Oh, an *artist*. Of course. Mike never told me that. He said you were a hospital administrator. You look,' he added candidly, 'like a hospital administrator.'

'Good,' said Penny.

He shook his head. 'You're the most perverse woman I've ever met.'

'I'm flattered,' Penny said sweetly.

'Yes, I can see that you would be.' He looked at her unflatteringly. 'Would you like me to pass that on to your mother as well?'

She did not react to the mockery. 'If you think it would be helpful,' Penny said with composure.

He looked bewildered. 'Helpful for what?'

So he was not going to admit the conspiracy. Well, she was not really surprised. She set her teeth.

'To stop her getting the wrong idea,' she snapped.

His brows twitched together. 'What sort of wrong idea?'

Penny hesitated. Then, 'That one wedding leads to another,' she said, goaded.

Zoltan stood rock-still.

'One——?'

'The wedding effect,' Penny said, remembering Sue Flynn. She clasped her arms in front of her, feeling suddenly cold.

'Ah. That effect.' He strolled over to the window and looked out into the dark copse that kept the kitchen shaded and cool.

'You've heard of it?'

He cast her an amused look over his shoulder.

'Hungary is no different from the rest of the world. At any wedding the old women are going round to the unmarried girls, saying, "Please God, your turn next." It's human nature.'

'Then human nature could do with some attention,' Penny muttered.

'Indubitably. However, you're in no danger from me. I'm not into marriage.' He sent her a wry look. 'And I like my affairs to be a little less of an assault course.'

She stared.

'I mean,' he said, his eyes glinting, 'that it takes more than twenty-four hours to seduce a porcupine. Even for one of my famous charm.' He smiled kindly. 'And, no matter what your family might have told you, I haven't got more than twenty-four hours. I've got a board meeting in Brussels on Monday and a lecture to prepare first. I only fitted in the wedding with a shoe-horn. So you can relax,' he added acidly. 'You're quite safe—at least from me.'

'Oh,' said Penny, fiercely embarrassed.

Zoltan did not notice. He was staring intently out of the window. He said with sudden urgency, 'Turn the light off.'

'*What*?'

'Lights. Out.'

She began to object. But there was something in his voice that demanded obedience. It went against all her instincts. Half resentful, she clicked the lights off. In the abrupt ensuing darkness she stood very still, suddenly a little afraid.

His voice was soft. 'You say everyone is out toasting the bride?'

'Everyone but you and me.' Her voice didn't sound like her own.

'So those characters crossing the lawn are not here by invitation?'

A hand motioned her imperatively. She saw the movement in the shadows. Her every instinct was to stand firmly where she was. But she had to know what he was looking at. Fuming inwardly, she went to his side. Her temper was not improved when, without hesitation, he took her hand and pointed it silently.

About to protest, Penny froze. He was perfectly right. There were three of them, moving quickly over the grass where the croquet hoops would be set up tomorrow. As far as she could make out they were wearing dark clothes. They were carrying sinister-looking bags, not unlike Zoltan's own.

He bent and said against her ear, 'Does anyone know you're here?'

He was too close, too comfortable with being too close—unlike herself. But now was hardly the time to say so. Swallowing, Penny shook her head. 'I don't know. Perhaps not. Mother probably said everyone was going out with Celia. I mean, she wouldn't think of saying I wasn't going because I never do.'

'So anyone who wanted to burgle the house would think it was empty tonight?'

Penny nodded. 'Except for the wedding presents.'

'What?'

'They're all laid out in the library. I told Mother it was silly and vulgar. But she said people liked to see their presents.'

'Valuable?'

She tried to think. 'I don't know. Some of them might be. Michael's very successful and his boss is rich. And Celia is a model. She's successful too. There could be some jewellery, I suppose. I don't take much notice...' She swallowed. 'The police. I'll call the police.'

He had not taken his eyes off the hurrying figures.

'You can try.'

He let go her hand and she flew across the kitchen, hardly noticing when she banged her hip painfully on the corner of the hall table. She lifted the phone off its cradle. There was no sound from it at all.

'Dead?' he asked softly.

Penny began to shake. 'Yes.'

'Any alternatives? Cellular phone? Car phone?'

She shook her head. 'My mother has one. But she'll have taken it with her. She always does.'

He did not waste time exclaiming.

'Where are those guys going, do you think? Straight to the room where the presents are?'

She went back to him, skirting the table more carefully this time. There was only one of the men visible now. She shuddered.

As if by instinct, a long arm came round her. Penny removed it.

'The famous charm working on autopilot?' she said acidly.

'Porcupine,' he said softly. Though there was a slight edge to it, she thought with satisfaction. 'Where?'

She tried to put herself in the burglars' place. 'N-not the study. It's on the first floor. Maybe the drawing-room. There are big French windows there. They wouldn't have to do any climbing.'

'Burglar alarm?'

'Not on,' Penny said. 'We're here, aren't we?'

'Yes, but they don't know that. So first they'll want to disable the burglar alarm,' he pointed out. 'Where is it?'

'The works, you mean? I'm not sure. They laid a cable through the flowerbed, I think...'

He moved, looked down at her in the darkness. 'Can you lock the drawing-room door into the hall?'

'Yes, but...'

'Let's get to it,' Zoltan said. 'While they're still cutting the wires of the burglar alarm.'

'But...'

'No, it won't stop them, or even hold them for long,' he murmured, as if he was agreeing with something she said. 'But it will buy some time while we think of what to do next.'

'*We*! Huh. So far all you've done is give me orders.'

'Don't be tiresome, there's a good girl,' he murmured.

'Tiresome——' Her voice began to rise.

He turned and kissed her rapidly on her open mouth. It was the briefest touch of the lips but its effect was electrifying. Penny gulped, gagged, and would have hit him—but he had already let her go.

'I know you're in shock. But save it for later.'

Zoltan was already moving to the kitchen door. He moved like a cat, silent-footed and neat. He motioned her past him and let her lead the way to the drawing-room. The door stood open on grey empty shadows. Silently he flowed past her and pulled the door shut, locking it with the heavy brass key. He took the key out and pocketed it, looking round.

Her father had bought a heavy refectory table which stood just inside the front door. Zoltan went to it, sized it up and then, to Penny's horror, flexed his shoulder muscles and picked it up.

He set it down across the door.

'A bit more time,' he said. She could hear the grin in his voice. He wasn't even breathing hard.

'Any more doors to the drawing-room?'

Penny hadn't thought of that. 'There's a sort of archway through to the dining-room. It's got a bookcase in it. You have to know that the bookcase is a door...'

'Sweetheart,' Zoltan said, 'whoever is out there, cutting the burglar alarm right now, has done their homework. Take me to the dining-room.'

Odious, superior man. And what made it worse was that he was right. Fuming, she went with him and they locked that door too. They piled the table and dining chairs up against it in a veritable obstacle course and she followed him back silently to the kitchen.

Once there, Zoltan locked that door too. He stood with his back to the door, listening.

Something nasty had just occurred to Penny. She said in a strangled voice, 'What if they've got guns?'

'Armed robbery?' Zoltan shook his head. 'Streets of New York, sure. Not a professional job in the English countryside.'

In spite of herself she moved closer. 'But——'

'You carry a gun if you think you're going to need it. You won't need it in an empty house. And if you did get caught, by some bad luck, then it would treble the sentence. Think about it, sweetheart,' he advised.

Penny was so offended by this casual lecture that she stopped trembling and stepped away from him. Zoltan, unaware, was concentrating on the problem in hand.

'Now, where did they come from?' he said in a musing tone.

Penny shuddered. 'You mean—are they local?' she said, bewildered.

'No, honey. I mean where have they left their wheels. They didn't walk here from the station,' he added drily. 'And they didn't drive up to the front door either.'

'Oh,' she said, enlightened. 'No, they wouldn't. There's a bell you set off if you come up the drive. The Warreners in Keepers' Cottage would hear it.' She thought about it, frowning. 'I suppose they could have come through the wood. There's a bridle-path of sorts.'

'Big enough for a van?' he asked swiftly.

Penny tried to remember. 'A small one. At least, I think so.'

'And they would have dumped the car in the wood, climbed through your hedge and come across the lawn,' Zoltan deduced.

Penny was beginning to see where this was leading.

'No, you can't,' she said in quick alarm. She was not talking about his theory. 'They could have left someone in the van on watch. They could come back. They could——'

'Hush.'

His fingers lay briefly against her cheek. Penny jumped. But this time she did not feel like protesting. Her heart was beating uncomfortably fast. Although they were speaking in whispers, she could still hear the amusement in his voice.

He said reasonably, 'Why should they have left anyone on guard? They don't know there's anyone in the house.'

Penny was beginning to shake again. 'They soon will,' she hissed. 'The moment they find that obstacle course we've just been building.'

'Which is why I must get to that van quickly,' Zoltan agreed coolly.

In the distance there was a crash, followed by the sound of tinkling glass.

'Well, they're in,' Zoltan said.

To Penny's amazement he sounded calm. No, more than calm—pleased. As if he was relishing the battle of wits. She strained to look up at him in the darkness. She could not make out his expression. But she could see the set of his jaw.

'*Please* don't go out there,' she said.

But he was withdrawing his arms, putting her away from him, moving catlike and silent to the kitchen door.

She flung herself after him. This time she managed to avoid the furniture. She hung on to his arm.

'You're not going out there without me,' she said in a ferocious whisper.

He looked down at her. 'You'll be perfectly safe...'

'I will. You won't.' She wanted to yell at him. It put a strain on her throat talking with this intensity at nil volume, she thought. 'It's just as much of an obstacle course out there, you know. Without me you'll fall into a ditch or something. Probably bring them on top of you. You need me. I'm coming. You can't stop me.'

He didn't want her to come. Penny could feel the resistance in the hard muscles bunching under her fingers. But he had not taught logic for nothing.

'OK,' he said reluctantly. 'But you do what I say. All right?'

'But——'

The arm under her hand was as unyielding as iron.

'All right?' he repeated softly.

Penny swallowed her protests. 'All right.'

'Come on, then.'

He possessed himself of her hand. She stiffened. He laughed under his breath.

'Can't afford to lose each other,' he murmured, taunting her. 'Still want to come?'

'I'm coming,' she said between gritted teeth.

His fingers tightened briefly on her own. Then he was letting them softly out of the back door. He was moving fast but he still took the time to put the deadbolt down behind them. No one was going to follow them that way. Penny realised with reluctant respect that she was in the hands of a man who didn't leave things to chance.

The back door opened on to a gravelled area. The crunching of their steps sounded appallingly loud to Penny, like gunshots in the dark. He stopped and pulled her close against him.

'We need to get on to grass, preferably under the trees, before we work our way round. Is that possible?'

She nodded. He put her gently in front of him.

'Show me.'

She led the way, her heart thumping. They tiptoed the three or four steps to the protection of the cherry tree.

'This is what we used to do as children,' Penny said. Her teeth were chattering. She felt cold and scared, disorientated and slightly disbelieving at the same time.

She gave a strained laugh. 'Playing highwaymen——'
Her voice started to rise.

Zoltan squeezed her hand. She subsided abruptly. She
stood beside him, quivering like a hunted animal. He
put an arm round her and held her against him strongly.
He did not speak. Penny took several long breaths. She
felt the frightening beginnings of hysteria dissolve.

'I'm sorry,' she muttered at last.

In the dark she felt him shrug—smile. How could you
feel a man smile in the dark? Penny thought. This was
crazy. But she could. It was like standing under a sun-
lamp.

'Nothing to be sorry about,' he murmured into her
ear. 'Ready to go on?'

She nodded, hoping he could not feel her expression
in his turn. Her lips were compressed into a tight line
and her jaw felt rigid with the effort of controlling her
alarm. She was not proud of herself. Who would believe
she was a cool, competent professional woman these days
if they could see her shivering like this?

He did not take her hand again. He let her lead the
way, skirting the lawn carefully in the deeper shadow
provided by the bushes and shrubs at the back of the
flowerbeds.

'Mr Lambton is going to go mad when he sees our
footprints all over his flowerbeds,' Penny muttered. 'He
moaned enough about the men who came to put up the
marquee. He's been getting the garden ready for the
wedding for weeks.'

Zoltan chuckled quietly. 'We all have our crosses to
bear.'

A crash came from the house. Penny looked over her
shoulder in alarm. The intruders had closed the curtains
in the drawing-room but it was clear that they had turned
the light on. From the sounds emerging into the still night
it was clear that they had discovered the barriers barring
their way out of the room. She shuddered a little.

Zoltan sent her a quick look, then overtook her and increased the pace. He had obviously identified the break in the hedge that she had been making for.

It was not easy scrambling under the tangled bushes in the dark. She got several scratches and more than a little debris in her hair and down her shirt. Zoltan set a punishing pace. She was soon breathing hard.

At the gap in the hedge he paused and reached back a hand to her. Penny took it thankfully. He vaulted lightly over the confining fence, half hidden by the greenery, and pulled her through after him.

Once in the wood he stood very still, looking round him. The shadows of the trees were enormous, engulfing them. Penny began to feel safer.

'Through there,' she said. 'That's the bridle-path.'

Zoltan had been right. As soon as they found the path they found the van. There had been no attempt to hide it in the undergrowth.

'They're confident,' Zoltan remarked.

He strolled round the van, trying its doors. The back one gave under very little pressure. It swung open with a grinding sound.

'Hinges want oiling,' Zoltan said critically.

He put one hand on the floor of the van and leaped up into it.

Penny thought about telling him to be careful and decided against it. She thought she had never in her life seen a man who looked more capable of taking care of himself. Or one less likely to be careful, she thought wryly.

He was making a thorough investigation of the van.

'Not very professional,' he said disapprovingly from its depths. 'Young and opportunist by the look of it. Certainly they have been drinking. No dedicated burglar would do that.'

He emerged clutching a couple of empty lager cans. Penny looked at them and winced.

'They're going to make a mess of the house, aren't they?' she said. 'If they're not professionals, I mean. They could get vindictive, couldn't they?'

'It's possible.'

'Oh, hell,' she said. 'That's all my mother needs, just before Celia's wedding. I wonder if there's a chance of leaving home before tomorrow.'

Zoltan laughed but he looked at her curiously.

'Your mother is not as philosophical as you, obviously.'

'She's spent a year getting ready for this wedding,' Penny said with feeling.

'Then we'd better stop them before they turn the place into a garbage tip,' he said lightly.

Penny stared, torn between hope and alarm. 'What do you mean? I thought we were going to make a break for it.'

He leaned up against the side of the van. He looked very tall in the moonlight-dappled shadows. There was a distinct breeze among the trees but he didn't seem aware of it. Penny shivered.

He seemed like one of the heroes out of legend, standing there. While she felt small and scared and very mortal.

'We have a choice,' Zoltan was saying. He did not sound in the least concerned. 'We can put the van out of action, get to your nearest neighbours and call the police.'

Penny swallowed. 'Or?'

'Or go back and stop any further mayhem,' he said tranquilly.

'Oh,' she said in a hollow voice.

She thought he was looking at her with a good deal of amused comprehension.

She was certain of it when he said, 'Or both.'

'How——?'

'You go for the phone,' he said gently. 'And I'll stop the riot.'

Penny was shaking her head even before he had finished speaking.

'That's ridiculous. You can't possibly go back in there on your own. There are at least three of them.'

In the dark she saw the wide shoulders lift in a shrug. She also made a discovery.

'You're enjoying yourself,' she said accusingly.

He did not try to deny it. 'Hell, I haven't had so much fun in years.'

Penny's tension found an entirely understandable release.

'You're completely irresponsible,' she raged, forgetting to keep her voice down in her exasperation. 'You're treating this whole thing as if you were a schoolboy. We should have run for help as soon as we saw them on the lawn.'

'I thought we were doing rather well,' Zoltan said mildly.

Penny glared at him. In the dark he could not see it, of course, but it relieved her feelings.

'This is not a *game*.'

'No, it's much more entertaining.'

She made a noise like a steam kettle coming to the boil. It surprised her. She had not made a noise like that since she was a child.

'Be serious.'

'OK,' he said, quite unoffended. 'Seriously, you head off to the friendly neighbours. And I'll have a chat with the boys about the error of their ways.'

'You are not going back to the house on your own,' Penny said positively.

'I'm quite able——'

'*No*,' she interrupted him.

'But by the time the police get here they could have spray-painted the drawing-room,' Zoltan pointed out.

'What do you think they'll do instead if you go down there on your own?' Penny flung at him. 'You don't *know* they're not armed.'

He shrugged again, laughing. 'Maybe with the odd beer can. I can handle that.'

She shuddered again. He would have seen that, she realised. Knowing he would have seen it—and had every right to think her the most appalling coward because of it—Penny could have screamed.

Instead she said tartly, 'Oh, can't you treat this seriously for a minute? We should both get out now.'

'And let your mother have hysterics all over your sister's wedding?' he challenged softly.

Penny was horribly torn. It was a choice between facing Laura Brinkman in despair or three drunken burglars, possibly armed. Neither prospect was attractive. But Laura's regrets, Penny thought, were likely to go on longer than any bruises would last. She made her decision.

'I'll come with you.'

He was startled. And not at all pleased, she thought.

'But——'

'I'm not arguing,' Penny said. 'Whatever we do, we do it together.'

There was a moment's silence while their wills met and clashed. The moon caught his hair, turning it to silver. In the shadows his eyes glinted like a sword-blade. She had the fancy that, just for that second, they were on another planet—heroic, alone and opposed, strangers who knew each other better than lovers. Penny's breath caught in her throat.

Then he gave a husky laugh.

'I'll remind you of that.'

'What?' So strong was the picture in her head that she barely registered what he said.

'Skip it. Not immediately relevant.'

She had the feeling that he was laughing at some private joke. She was about to demand enlightenment when across the distant lawn the lights of the drawing-room seemed to blaze briefly. She stared. He followed her eyes.

'Ah,' he said with satisfaction. 'Developments.'

Penny swallowed. There was a figure on the lawn. It was not particularly furtive but it was moving fast. It was coming directly for the place where they stood in the shadow of the van.

'Now, that,' said Zoltan in his lazy, laughing voice, 'is very helpful.'

'Helpful?' Penny gasped.

'Divide and rule,' he reminded her. 'Back into the bushes with you.'

She did not protest. She might not understand what Zoltan was doing but it was only too clear that he knew exactly. At his silent gesture, she retreated into the wood. She found a friendly witch hazel and huddled under the slender branches, breathing in the fragrance of its blossom without appreciation. She looked back at the van.

Zoltan was nowhere to be seen. But the door at the back was swinging slightly. They must have forgotten to close it, Penny thought in sudden anguish. She measured the distance. Was there time for her to close it before the intruder came through the hedge?

But no. He was there already, climbing over the drunken fence. He did not even pause when he saw the open door. He climbed straight into the vehicle and began to rummage noisily.

Penny saw a shadow move below the van. Or did she? Surely—yes—or——?

Her heart was thundering. She put a hand to her side to ease the pain of a stitch. Her eyes stared till they ached. Then she saw it again.

Zoltan's long-legged figure stepped silently out of the shadows. The man was getting clumsily out of the van, carrying an armful of tools that looked heavy. Zoltan's arm flicked sideways. Penny's hands flew to her mouth. The man fell without making a sound. There was a muted grunt from Zoltan as he fielded the tools.

Carefully he put the tools on the ground. Then he was down on one knee by the intruder, efficiently removing his belt and using it to tie the man's hands behind his back.

Penny came out from under the witch hazel at a running crouch.

'What have you done?' she hissed.

He turned towards her and put a finger to his lips. His eyes glittered in the moonlight.

'You've hurt him,' she accused in a furious whisper.

'He'll live,' he whispered back.

He didn't sound either regretful or worried, Penny noticed.

'There was no need for violence.'

He sent her an ironical look. But all he said was, 'Open the van doors,' in the same indifferent tone.

He hefted the man to his feet and then tipped the dangling body over his shoulder. He looked down at Penny.

'He'll be more comfortable lying down,' he said mockingly.

Her lips tightened. She turned on her heel and flung open the van doors with an exaggerated bow.

'Thank you.'

He stepped up into the van without any apparent effort at all. He must be immensely strong, Penny thought. For some reason it was not as comforting a reflection as she might have expected.

He laid down his burden and just turned the man's head, checking his breathing. Satisfied, he stepped lithely down on to the moss-covered path.

'One down,' he said lightly, 'two to go. Back to your foxhole and see what we get next.'

Penny went. She thought his flippancy deplorable and his attitude downright dangerous but now was not the time to say so. Or indeed, anything. So she went.

For an age, it seemed, nothing else happened. Penny became aware of the breeze turning to a cold wind as clouds covered the moon. She wished she were nearer to Zoltan; or even that she knew where he was.

Nothing stirred in the wood except branches and small nocturnal animals, cheeping and squeaking as they scuttled about their business. She might have been alone. For a moment she even wondered if he had left her in the wood while he went back to the house in pursuit of the other intruders. But even as she started to straighten and peer about her, she realised that he would not abandon her.

It was odd that she should be so certain of it, Penny thought with a slight shock. But she was. Truly as if they were strangers who knew the depths of each other's hearts.

That is crazy, she said to herself.

She had no time to ponder further, however, because there was activity coming from the house again. This time there were two of them. And they were not just trotting across the lawn to fetch a crowbar. They were moving with a silent purposefulness that made Penny press her knuckles hard against her teeth to suppress a whimper of dismay.

They came over the fence cautiously, one looking round, guarding the other. Zoltan would not be able to step up behind these two and knock them senseless. They backed round the van, their eyes darting, their backs tight against the vehicle's sides. They looked fit and ready to take on anyone.

But that was not the worst of it. They had things in their hands. At first Penny thought they were tools of some sort—maybe a spanner or a wrench. Then, turning cold to the marrow of her bones, she realised what they were. She had never, she thought with a sort of detached despair, seen a gun in real life before.

Please let Zoltan keep down and let them go, she prayed silently. I wish we'd never started this. I wish I'd insisted on going for the police. I wish——

And then one of the shadows moved. Penny's teeth drew blood. She wanted to close her eyes, to shut out the carnage she was sure would follow. But she could not.

With a start she realised that there was now three figures stepping warily round the van, their backs pressed against it. As she watched disbelievingly one of them seemed to touch the other on the shoulder and, as he turned, fell him with one of those silent, horizontal blows she had seen before. Penny winced—but this time she did not protest.

Suddenly the stalking silence was broken. The van began to bang and rock as if of its own accord. With a start she realised that Zoltan's prisoner must have recovered consciousness. The two circling figures were both plainly startled by the commotion. One turned and was face to face with the other. Penny saw him raise the thing that was not a spanner.

Without thinking, she was hurtling out from under the witch hazel, screaming.

The gun froze, shifted, turned in her direction, shifted again uncertainly. It happened in a split-second but it was long enough. The other shadow flung itself upon him and they were grappling, rolling to and fro among the moss and leaf-mould.

There was another gun, Penny thought frantically. When the other man went down he had been carrying a gun. Desperate, she looked round.

Some accident of the moonlight caught a dull gleam. She made a dive. It was a cold, ugly thing but she scrabbled it up and held it to her breast as tight as a favourite bear.

Someone was coming off very much the worst in the tangle of arms and legs on the ground. Penny thought longingly of Keeper's Cottage, the Warreners and their telephone. But she could not leave Zoltan. He might need her. Or at least her weapon—if she could make a convincing display of knowing how to fire it.

There was an ugly series of grunts. Then a thump. One man fell back. The arms and legs resolved themselves into two figures, one unmoving. A tall shadow unfolded himself and stood up. He looked down at the prone body.

Penny groped for a decent hold on the gun. The man did not turn his head. He seemed unaware of her.

She swallowed and turned the gun.

'Don't shoot,' said Zoltan Guard, a grin in his voice. 'There's quite enough cleaning up to be done before the wedding already.'

She jumped. She let the gun fall with equal relief and fury.

'You——'

'Give me your belt, sweetheart. I need to tie these monkeys up.'

She fumbled the required article out of its confining loops one-handed. The gun bumped against her thigh.

He took the belt, trussed up the two men on the ground, and came back to her.

'Is there any other item of my clothing you would like?' Penny asked icily. She was shivering uncontrollably but she was damned if she was going to let him see it.

He grinned. She saw the gleam of his teeth in the moonlight.

'Not just at the moment.' He put a hand out and tipped her chin to look up at him.

I am an adult, independent woman, Penny thought incredulously. How dare he pinch my chin as if I'm a schoolgirl? How can I be so stupid as to stand here and let him?

She removed his hand and stepped back. Unfortunately, she had forgotten the gun. It banged against her leg, causing her to stumble. Zoltan reached down his other hand and hefted it easily out of her grasp.

'Mrs Brinkman,' he murmured, 'if this is your boring daughter I don't think I can cope with the others.'

And, to Penny's silent outrage, for the third time that night, he brushed laughing lips against her own.

CHAPTER FOUR

PENNY stood very still. There was the same electric tingle, unwelcome but unmistakable. From the gleam in the blue eyes Zoltan Guard was well aware of her reaction. She winced at the thought as at the flick of a whip.

'I must call the police,' she said briskly, stepping away from him.

Even with the distance of several feet between them, she could still feel the warmth of his lips. She was dismayed. In the moonlit wood he looked impossibly attractive. Something inside her reached out to him. I don't want this, Penny thought. Just the possibility, the imagination of attraction made her wince as if at the touch of fire. She saw him take note of it.

But all he said was, 'Good thinking, Batwoman.'

He glanced at the bodies on the ground. One of them was stirring with a groan.

'I'll lock these beauties in the van. Then I'll join you.'

He did. But not before Penny had spoken to a bored duty officer who suddenly became a lot less bored at her news.

'Sounds as if you got a regular little gang there, Mrs Dane,' he said approvingly. 'Hang on.' There were some clicks on the line and he came back to her. 'The first car should be with you in ten minutes.'

It was six. The police arrived just after Zoltan had strolled back into the kitchen. It seemed natural that he went out to meet them. Even more natural that he took them over to the van. But it did nothing for Penny's temper. Here he was taking matters out of her hands again, she thought, irritated.

71

She set to work dismantling their makeshift barriers, pulling the furniture back into place with an energy born of a rising fury.

By the time Zoltan and the senior policeman came back to the house the rooms were restored to their previous order and Penny was hot, dusty and spitting mad.

Zoltan identified her mood at once; she saw from the way his mouth tilted. It did not placate her.

'Mrs Dane can tell you more about what happened than I can, Sergeant,' he said smoothly. 'I'm only a visitor. She was the one who realised the gang must be after the wedding presents. And she worked out where their transport had to be parked. I just—er—provided a helping hand.'

The sergeant was not deceived by this modesty. Nor was Penny. Zoltan's intention to keep her sweet was blatant, she thought. She ground her teeth.

But, in the face of this graceful acknowledgement, she could do nothing except be gracious in her turn. Or not if she wanted to keep any semblance of dignity. Oh, he was an expert manipulator, she thought, seething.

'Trapping the burglars was entirely Professor Guard's work,' she said curtly.

The sergeant smiled. He had clearly never thought anything else. He sent the odious man a look of admiration.

'I'll need a statement from you, sir. And you as well, of course, Mrs Dane.'

Zoltan looked down at her. There was a gleam in his eye that the innocent sergeant must have thought was solicitude. Penny, seeing the gleam under the downswept lashes, knew different.

'Of course. But not tonight, mmm? It's been fairly stressful. And Mrs Dane has had a shock.'

He put an arm round her waist. It was more of a challenge than a support. But the policeman did not know that. He gave a sentimental sigh and nodded.

Penny whisked herself out of the provocative embrace.

'I have had no bigger a shock than you have,' she told Zoltan coldly. 'I'm perfectly capable of giving the police a statement about what happened.'

The sergeant said soothingly, 'No need to worry about that tonight, Mrs Dane. We've got enough to hold those three varmints. Your boyfriend's identified them.'

Penny stiffened. Zoltan's face was an elaborate mask of innocence. The sergeant did not notice. He was chuckling reminiscently.

'Bit of a formality, that, seeing as they were tied up with your belts. Still, that's all we need to charge them tonight. Someone will be down to take a detailed statement later. Probably next week some time.' He looked at his watch. 'But no need to keep you good people from your bed any longer. You'll be glad of your rest tonight,' he added. 'Shock's a funny thing. Takes people different ways. You want to treat it with respect. Well, I'll say goodnight.'

Penny said nothing. Zoltan, after a quick look at her, said goodnight for both of them and showed the helpful sergeant out.

He came back to the drawing-room, eyeing her warily.

'My *boyfriend*?' Penny's harsh question was an accusation in itself.

Zoltan's lips twitched. 'An understandable mistake,' he murmured.

'Not unless that's what you told him. Did you?'

'Now, why would I do that?' He sounded hurt.

'I don't think there's anything you wouldn't do if you thought it was funny,' Penny said grimly. '*Did* you?'

He shrugged. 'He may have assumed something. It hardly seemed necessary to take him into the exact nature of our relationship.'

'We do not have a relationship,' Penny said in a strangled voice.

'Well, quite.' One eyebrow flicked up. His smile was bland. 'But it would only have confused him if I'd said that, wouldn't it?'

She glared at him, unable to deny his reasoning, but deeply suspicious of it at the same time.

His voice grew coaxing. 'Look, the man was here to collect some criminals. If he finds a man and a woman alone in the house and jumps to the obvious conclusion, what does it matter? He will have forgotten it as soon as he gets back and starts writing out the charge sheets.'

Penny said between her teeth, 'It was not the obvious conclusion. I——'

The smile was back in his eyes. 'Oh, yes, it was,' he said gently.

The indignant words died on her lips. 'What?' she said blankly.

'He's a good detective, your policeman. He picked it up at once.'

Penny did not believe it. He could not be saying what he seemed to be saying. The shock-induced anger leaked away. It was replaced by something much more complicated. Though it probably did nothing for her shock levels, she thought wryly.

'I don't understand,' she said, hoping she was telling the truth. If her suspicions were right she was heading into a situation she had not foreseen, much less invited, and she did not have the faintest idea how she was going to handle it.

'No, I know you don't.' Zoltan's expression was thoughtful. 'I find that—intriguing.'

Somewhere deep in her breast Penny's heart closed up tight like a threatened sea anemone. The tension under her ribcage was so fierce it almost hurt. Involuntarily, she put a hand to her side, to ease the vestigial pain.

She was hardly aware she was doing it. Zoltan was aware, though. She saw one eyebrow flick up in a curious expression of disbelief, almost of regret. Following his glance, she dropped her hand to her side again swiftly.

'What do you mean?' she said, not really wanting an answer.

In the same gentle tone he said, 'It's not just the skin and the dangerous green eyes, you know.'

She shook her head. 'I don't know what you're talking about.'

'I'm afraid you do. You may not understand it. But you know what I'm talking about, all right.' He was not laughing any more. If anything, he sounded almost grim.

Penny turned a shoulder and began to push a brocade sofa back into place.

'You're wrong,' she said over her shoulder. 'I haven't the slightest idea.'

She lined the sofa up in its former position, plumped up the cushions and straightened, ignoring him. The picture above it had been knocked crooked, she saw. She began to straighten that too.

A long arm came over her shoulder. She went very still. Zoltan eased the dipping corner of the picture until the bottom edge was precisely horizontal. She could feel the warmth of his unhurried breathing on the back of her neck. It was disturbing.

'Look at me.'

'I——'

'Don't dare?' he taunted softly.

Penny's chin lifted at that. She whipped round, prepared to tell him that she was very happy to dare anything he could challenge her with. It was a tactical error. Powerful arms closed round her before her confused brain had even managed to register how much too close he was.

Too close and too gorgeous. And he knew it. The unquestioning confidence was there in the easy way he held her, the laughing mouth, the arrogant tilt of the head. Registering all that amused assurance with a sinking heart, Penny suddenly saw something else as well: a tiny flame in the blue eyes.

As she stared up at him in bemusement it flickered into hot life. His arms tightened, jerking her against his muscular length. She gasped.

Which meant her lips were already parted when his mouth closed over hers. And this time it was not a kiss without passion—on either side, Penny realised with a slight shock.

They were so close that she could feel his heart thudding, his blood drumming in his veins. She could feel, too, that for all that magnificent assurance he was trembling very slightly. And, for all her anger, she was trembling even harder and clinging to him as she had never clung to anyone in the whole of her life.

Without lifting his mouth from hers he turned their locked bodies until they collapsed on to the sofa. Penny thought he gave a breathless laugh at the success of the manoeuvre. It sounded triumphant. That should have ignited her anger again—or at least put her on her guard. But it did not.

Lying among the cushions, she snaked her arms round his neck and kissed him with a demand as great as his own. It set him on fire. The grip of his arms relaxed. Then his hands became imperious. Penny gave a soundless gasp. She arched to a searching sensuality she had never imagined in her wildest dreams. She was beyond remembering, beyond thinking at all—except of how exquisitely gentle his touch was.

She began to shiver like her childhood pony before a horse show—half excited, half terrified. It made her cling to him all the harder, her eyes tight shut.

He was saying something in a language she did not recognise, crooning it against her skin as his kisses travelled. His bent head pushed aside the tangled shirt. Without her realising what was happening he had already dealt with the buttons. Now he was pulling aside her fragile underwear. She felt his mouth on her breast. It was a sensation like drowning. She arched into it, wanting to lose herself in that lovely oblivion.

But something was wrong. Something was happening. The darkness behind her tight-shut eyelids was shot across with lightning. In the distance there was the noise of a car engine . . . a voice . . .

Penny surfaced reluctantly. Zoltan muttered a protest against her skin, not stirring. Penny looked down at the gleaming head against her pale naked flesh and blushed wildly. She began to struggle.

His hands tightened. 'No . . .'

'Someone's arrived,' she hissed.

For a moment she thought he was not going to let her up. She had a brief, startling vision of her mother and sister walking into the drawing-room to find her half-undressed wrapped around a stranger. It brought her back to reality as nothing else could have done.

'Let me up,' she said frantically, beginning to push at him.

For just another second he resisted. Then a door banged, unmistakably.

Zoltan raised his head and inspected her flushed face.

Desperately embarrassed, Penny struggled with underwear. She pulled at the cotton shirt to very little effect. It must have wound itself round her while she writhed in his arms, she thought, wincing.

'Please.'

He lifted himself off her then, sat her up and buttoned the shirt swiftly round her. As if she were about six, Penny thought. She was irrationally annoyed at the alacrity with which he obeyed her.

'If this is another burglar, the police should start giving you a discount for bulk purchase,' he murmured, getting to his feet.

Penny followed suit. She tugged at the waistband of her trousers, which had unaccountably come undone.

'It will be my father. I recognise his voice.' Her voice sounded stiff and unnatural in her ears.

She did not look at him. She could not. She was still trembling to the core from that sensual onslaught.

Zoltan, however, seemed unmoved. 'The great actor?'

She nodded. He smiled. Even without looking at him she knew he was smiling, amused.

'I don't think much of his timing,' he said drily.

Penny blushed fierily. Zoltan's eyes narrowed.

'Do you want me to head him off?'

She stared, uncomprehending.

'While you—er—tidy yourself up,' he explained.

She winced again. No doubt he was seeing what anyone would see—a tremulous mouth and a dazed, dazzled look. She knew that look. She had seen it in the mirror every night when she was first in love with Alan. There was even a mirror above the fireplace now. Out of the shadows her haunted face looked back at her.

What is happening to me? He doesn't want an affair any more than I do. He just uses that damned charm of his without noticing.

Except that he had noticed the effect it had on her, Penny thought. And had pursued his advantage ruthlessly. She looked at him now. In the semi-dark he was laughing, relaxed, unconcerned. But he had not been unconcerned when she was in his arms just now. So why had he kissed her? *Why?*

He reached out a hand to her but she brushed it away, straightening her clothes with fingers that still shook.

'I'm fine,' she said, shaking her head. 'Fine.'

'Penny——'

She could not bear any more of that meaningless, too-powerful charm. She brushed past him. Head high, she went back to the kitchen. Just in time, as it turned out.

The kitchen door banged back on its hinges. A strong breeze sent a flurry of fallen wistaria blossom across the floor. Behind them appeared a wavering shadow.

'I'm home,' sang out the intruder.

Two matching suitcases were dumped inside the door and a tall figure followed them in, weaving slightly. He made two or three passes at the outer door before managing to close it.

'Hello-oo.'

Zoltan was at her shoulder. He held her strongly. She could feel his heart beating in steady hammer-blows under her shoulderblade. A long sweet shiver went up her spine. She fought it.

'Let me go. My father will see.'

He said in her ear, 'You're joking. He'd be lucky to see an oak tree in that state.'

'What?'

'The father of the bride,' he said, with an edge to the even tone, 'has obviously been celebrating. Unlike her sister.' He let her go.

Penny bit her lip. She went to her father's side and slipped an unobtrusively supporting hand under his elbow.

'Hello, Charles. I thought you were staying in London tonight.'

'Too noisy.'

He allowed himself to be guided to the kitchen table. He surveyed its forgotten contents and his face brightened.

'Wine.' He reached for the bottle.

Zoltan, laughing again, found a glass and poured it for him.

'Thankee,' said Charles Brinkman in his best stage pirate.

Penny made sure that he was propped against the table before she removed her hand. Coffee, she could see, was required. Lots of it and fast. He needed to be sobered up before her mother and sister got back.

Charles took a long swig of wine. Then, registering that the friendly face was not familiar, he lowered his glass. A look of confusion crossed the famously handsome features.

'Which one are you?'

Zoltan smiled. 'Which what?'

'Son-in-law,' explained Charles Brinkman.

To Penny's acute eye, Zoltan shuddered. But he said politely enough, 'I'm afraid I don't have that honour.'

Charles nodded sagely. 'Too many son-in-laws,' he remarked in self-pitying tones which made it all too clear, if that had been necessary, that the wine was not his first beverage of the evening.

Zoltan chuckled. 'Comes with the territory. So many gorgeous daughters,' he explained as Charles looked puzzled.

Charles looked vaguely round the kitchen. His look of puzzlement deepened when his gaze fell on Penny. She flinched. All it needed to close a perfect evening was for her father to explain why this particular daughter had provided the worst possible candidate in the way of sons-in-law, she thought savagely.

'Hadn't you better go to bed and sleep it off, Charles?' she snapped before he could speak.

Zoltan's eyes narrowed. But Charles beamed.

'That's my girl. You always look after me. Always look after all of us...' He was becomingly muzzily sentimental.

Penny said crisply, 'If you don't go to bed now you'll be caught by Mother and the bridesmaids.'

It worked. He heaved himself to his feet, reaching absent-mindedly for the bottle. Penny removed it from his grasp. She replaced it with a bottle of mineral water from the fridge.

She could feel Zoltan watching her, watching Charles. She urged her father to the door.

'Don't forget to drink the water,' she instructed. 'If you have a hangover tomorrow Mother will never forgive you. Especially if you mess up your speech.'

He looked at her reproachfully. 'Never fluffed a speech in my life.'

But he stuffed the plastic bottle under his arm and went out. Penny listened as he tacked noisily up the stairs. She heaved a sigh of relief.

Zoltan said, 'You got rid of him very summarily.'

She was startled. 'I'm sorry?'

'Didn't even tell him about our adventurous evening. Just packed the poor old guy off to bed.' He leaned against the kitchen wall and folded his arms over his chest, inspecting her. 'Don't you like your family?'

For no reason that she could think of, Penny found herself flushing. 'Don't be ridiculous,' she said.

His eyes were searching. And not laughing any more.

'They want a lot of sustaining,' she burst out under that dispassionate gaze. 'A lot of attention. It's sometimes more than I can bear.'

'You don't know how lucky you are to have anything to bear at all,' Zoltan said softly. 'I can't remember the last time I saw my father. And as for my mother——' He shrugged. 'She never bothered where I was or with whom. Even when I was half a world away. And here you are, all set to go to war because you think your family want to fix you up with an escort so you can have a nice time at your sister's wedding.'

Put like that it sounded petty in the extreme. Penny was torn between indignation and a weird desire to vindicate herself, to wipe that look of lurking contempt out of his eyes. Indignation won, but only just.

'What is it to do with you?' she said heatedly.

'Well, you seem quite clear that I've been elected the escort under reference,' he drawled. 'So you might say I have a vested interest.'

She said between her teeth, 'You have no interest in me. Nor I in you.'

'You keep saying that.'

'Because it's true.' He looked sceptical. Her temper rose a notch. 'It's self-evident.'

He shook his head. 'If it were self-evident you wouldn't have to say it.'

'I keep saying it,' said Penny, with desperate calm, 'because you seem to need reminding of it.' She added waspishly, 'Which, given your views on affairs, I find hard to account for.'

His mouth slanted. 'I have nothing against affairs. I just don't like to rush them.'

Penny met his eyes and found them quizzical. The contempt had not exactly gone but it had been pushed to one side, she thought, temporarily put on one side while Zoltan amused himself baiting her. She wished he did not have such instant success in doing so.

She said, 'Well, that rules me out, doesn't it?'

'Not,' he said, 'necessarily.' He strolled forward.

Penny became horribly aware of her heart racing. The blood pounded so loudly in her ears that she was afraid he would hear it. She remembered, all too vividly, how she had writhed in his arms.

She retreated behind a chair with more prudence than dignity and spoke rapidly.

'I know I went a bit crazy before my father arrived but you have to believe that was completely out of character. You said yourself, I was in shock.'

'Yes,' he agreed in a thoughtful tone, 'I think you were.'

Penny looked at him uneasily. There was something in his tone that she was sure would be unwelcome if she could only fathom it.

'What do you mean?' she said suspiciously.

His smile had a hard edge. 'That for an experienced woman, which I take you to be, you are extraordinarily reluctant to recognise your own feelings.'

Her hands clenched hard by her sides. Realising, she straightened them quickly.

'You're imagining it,' she said curtly.

'I don't think so.'

'I was in shock because of an armed burglary,' Penny declared, her voice rising. 'I had every reason——'

'You were in shock because you were responding to me,' he said quietly. 'Until your father arrived you'd forgotten where we were and you didn't know what was going to happen next. What's more, you didn't care.'

Penny stood very still. 'No,' she said in a voice of horror.

He just looked at her, faintly frowning.

'No.'

'You need to take a good long look at your feelings, I think.'

She swallowed. All the same she managed to send him a hard, defiant look.

'And what feelings are those?'

'Attraction, excitement . . .'

She shrank. It was all horribly familiar. That was what Alan had offered, demanded, imposed . . . She shut her eyes. Oh, God!

But Zoltan Guard did not know any of that and she was not about to tell him.

She pulled herself together and said with rather shaky sarcasm, 'You flatter yourself.'

'. . . set against fear and cowardice.'

That was safer ground. Penny glared at him. 'Are you calling me a coward?'

'Yup.'

She thought of the horrors of her marriage, of the irascible consultants that only she could deal with, of the life she had built out of devastation.

'You're crazy,' she said calmly. 'No one's ever called me a coward.'

He was watching her with an odd little smile. 'OK. Prove it.'

'I don't have to——' She stopped.

His smile grew. He did not say, Point proven. He did not have to. Those weary blue eyes said it for him.

It was like conceding him the victory without even attempting to fight. Penny's self-respect could not endure it. She took a deep breath.

'How?'

The steep lids fell. 'Come to bed with me,' Zoltan Guard said gently.

CHAPTER FIVE

THERE was a moment when Penny thought she had not heard properly. She shook her head, trying to rid it of the distortion through which her own subconscious mind must have filtered his words. An embarrassing distortion—and worrying evidence of exactly what was preoccupying her subconscious mind, she thought, disturbed.

Then, slowly, she realised that Zoltan had said exactly what she thought he had said. And the sheer outrageousness of it silenced her. She stared at him, her brain whirling.

One dark eyebrow flicked up. 'There's no need to look so dismayed. It was an offer, not a command.'

An *offer*. Penny stared at him for a disbelieving moment. Just for a moment she had a vivid picture of herself entwined with those strong limbs, all that electric concentration bent on her and her alone. Her breath shivered in her throat.

And then common sense reasserted itself. Along with it, for the first time that night, came her sense of humour. It was a huge relief. Penny pushed a hand through her hair and looked at him wryly.

'I can't believe you said that.' The germ of a laugh quivered in her voice.

Zoltan's eyes narrowed. 'Believe it.'

'I'd rather not,' Penny said firmly. 'You've embarrassed me quite enough for one evening.'

'How have I embarrassed you?'

She looked at him speechlessly. Then irrepressible laughter began to bubble up. If there was a faint note of controlled hysteria in it, he failed to point it out. And Penny herself was beyond noticing.

Zoltan watched her without comment, his eyes hooded. At last she choked to a halt. She rummaged for a handkerchief, failed to find one, and mopped her eyes on the back of her hand, looking round for the roll of kitchen paper. Finding it, she tore off a sheet and blew her nose vigorously.

'I'm sorry. I shouldn't——' The convulsive laughter threatened again and she drew a steadying breath. 'It's just that this is all slightly outside my experience. And when you asked how you'd embarrassed me——' She broke off, strangled, and blew her nose again.

'Outside my experience too,' Zoltan said with a hint of crispness. 'I've never had a lady laugh in my face before.'

'Oh. I'm sorry.' Penny was genuinely taken aback. She was even briefly contrite. 'I didn't mean to be rude.'

He was indifferent. 'My ego will stand it.'

It sounded as if it would too. Her contrition dwindled somewhat.

He was looking at her with that curiously detached interest again.

'But I'm still interested in the answer. Does sexual attraction embarrass you, then?'

What was left of her contrition contracted to a microdot and disappeared.

'It must be perfectly obvious what embarrassed me,' she countered swiftly. 'The same as would embarrass any other halfway sensible person. Or do you normally ask women to bed the first time you meet them?'

His eyebrows flew up. There was an odd expression on his face; it almost looked as if she had startled him. But then that lazy self-possession took over again.

'Depends on the woman. And the time,' he drawled.

Penny looked at him levelly. 'Another old Hungarian custom?'

He laughed aloud at that. 'Honey, I've been out of Hungary a long time. I learned my courting rituals on the Californian beaches.'

So that accounted for the accent, Penny thought. And the tan. And other things.

'I see where you get your high embarrassment threshold,' she told him affably.

He shrugged. 'Embarrassment is a waste of time. You want something, you go for it. Maybe you get hurt.' Under the lazy eyelids, the glance he bent on her was keen. 'Getting hurt is a pain. But it's better than letting embarrassment bounce you out of trying.'

Penny shook her head. 'Good try,' she said. 'The answer is still no.'

'Yes, I can see it is,' he agreed without apparent concern. 'I'm still interested in why.'

She hesitated. It must be her tiredness—or some odd integrity that she sensed in him that demanded honesty—but suddenly she wanted to tell him the truth. Suddenly serious, a little shy, she said, 'Have you ever been in love, Zoltan?'

His body seemed to tense.

'Yes.'

'Often?'

'Enough.'

'Well, I've only been in love once. I was nineteen and I wanted to give him the moon. I did my best to. Everybody said I was crazy and he—didn't want the moon anyway. The trouble was we found it out too late.'

Zoltan was very still. 'That's why you're embarrassed?' He sounded disbelieving.

Penny shook her head. 'That's why I'm out of the game.' She hesitated. 'I've played all my chips, you see. There's nothing left. There hasn't been ever since. I suppose I'm a one-man girl who chose the wrong man. My family all think I should try again. But I know—

I'm not like that.' She looked him bravely in the face. 'Can you understand that?'

He said in a strange voice, 'Nobody ever since? One throw and that was it?'

Penny nodded.

'You're right,' he said with feeling. 'Your family don't understand you. That was one hell of a gamble.'

'I know now. I didn't at nineteen.'

'So now you don't take any risks at all.' He paused, watching her face. Then he diagnosed slowly. 'I'd say a green-eyed blonde who looks like you and doesn't take risks gets embarrassed a hell of a lot.'

She smiled a little. 'No, I can usually deflect anything that looks potentially embarrassing. You've given me more sticky moments this evening than I've had in the last five years put together.'

'So I've shaken you up after all?' He did not sound particularly pleased with his victory.

There was no point in lying. He was too shrewd. Anyway she was too emotionally drained. Her chin lifted. 'Yes.'

He said nothing. There was a brooding expression in the blue eyes. Her chin came down.

'Not a great evening one way and another,' she said ruefully. 'And one hell of a day coming. I don't know about you, but I need my sleep. Do you want anything else before I go to bed?'

Even as she said it, she thought, That could have been better phrased. But he did not take it up, make a joke. In fact he ignored it.

'So I've shaken you up.' The self-mockery was almost bitter. 'Well, at least you can comfort yourself that it's mutual,' he said harshly.

That shook her out of her weary calm. Her eyes flew to his, shocked.

'Oh, yes,' he said, with more than a touch of grimness. 'I'll go off to bed like a gentleman and I won't come creeping round your door—even if I knew which it was. But don't think either of us is going to sleep tonight. Because we won't.'

He was right, of course.

Penny tucked herself into the single bed she had had from childhood and, for the first time in her life, could not get comfortable in it. She tossed and turned, lost her bedcovers, knocked over her alarm clock, heard the bridesmaids' party returning...

In the end Penny gave up and turned the light on. It was three o'clock. She shivered. Although it was nearly summer, the dead hour of the night was as cold as December.

She remembered Zoltan's strictures on the English climate. Was he, too, awake and cold in his room under the eaves?

She hugged her arms round herself. What on earth had possessed her to tell him so much? It was more than she had ever told her concerned family, more than she had said to any of the occasional boyfriends who took her out to dinner from time to time and ended up wondering vainly why they never got any closer. More even than she had told Sue Flynn, the friend and confidante who knew more about her than anyone else.

Yet here she was spilling it all out to Zoltan Guard like an adolescent on a radio phone-in, she thought, disgusted with herself. I was nineteen. I was in love. There's nothing left. God, it was pathetic. How he must be laughing at her if he was awake.

She pulled the blanket up round her shoulders against the cold. Would she have been warmer in Zoltan's arms? It was an involuntary thought and it shocked her. But once it was there she could not quite banish it at once. Would she have felt happier? Safer? Or once more terrifyingly at risk? Once she had dreamed of sleeping

in Alan's arms, cherished and secure. And look what
had happened to that.

Penny shook her head, banishing the traitorous
thoughts. More of the wedding effect, she told herself
grimly. She had not imagined herself in a man's arms
since long before Alan left. Now was not a good time
to start. At least if she wanted to retain her peace of
mind. There were safer ways of getting warm.

She got out of bed, found bedsocks and an old velvet
dressing-gown and climbed back into bed. Even so, it
was not until the light began to show grey round the
wistaria leaves outside her window that she finally slept.

Inevitably perhaps, she was late for breakfast. She had
dark circles under her eyes and a tense look about the
jaw that, she knew, was all too likely to give rise to
comment. She paused in the doorway, bracing herself.
Everyone else was already there.

Laura looked up, her eyes preoccupied. 'Morning,
darling. Overslept?'

Penny nodded, relieved. Normally her mother would
have demanded an immediate explanation of her washed-
out appearance and uncharacteristically late arrival at
the breakfast table.

Zoltan looked up quickly. She saw him take in the
signs of sleeplessness at once. His mouth tightened.

He was looking good. No signs of a bad night there,
Penny thought ruefully, in spite of what he had said last
night. She did not know whether to be glad or sorry.

There was an empty seat opposite him. She slipped
into it, not quite meeting his eyes. They were alert. They
swept over her in a comprehensive survey that brought
a faint colour to her cheeks.

Fortunately her mother did not notice that either. She
was pouring coffee. She handed it across to Penny.

'The flowers haven't arrived,' she said in a distracted
way. 'I've phoned the florist but they don't answer.'

Charles snorted. 'There were half a dozen women taking whole trees into the marquee when I came down,' he said.

Laura shook her head. 'That's the Women's Institute. They are doing the marquee and the church. I *told* you, Charles. The florist from London is supposed to be doing the flowers in the drawing-room and all the bouquets. It's *Jennings'* present to Celia.'

'Then they won't have forgotten, will they?' Charles said reasonably. 'A London florist isn't going to forget a top fashion magazine's order for flowers for a top model's wedding, are they? Too much free publicity,' he added with professional sympathy.

Laura ignored that. She did not like the more commercial aspects of her beautiful daughter's wedding. On the whole she had been fairly successful in pretending they did not exist so far, Penny thought with amused affection. But if Charles, less sentimental about these matters, started rubbing it in, he would find himself with a full-scale row on his hands. Laura was already pretty wrought-up, she thought.

She said in her quiet voice, 'When did you call them, Mother?'

Charles gave another of his massive snorts.

'She's been doing it every hour on the hour since the dawn chorus started. I'm not surprised they haven't phoned her back.'

Laura looked as if she might cry. 'Well, florists have to get up early to go to market to buy the flowers.'

'If they're still buying the flowers the blasted things aren't going to be sitting here in the drawing-room with bows in their hair, are they?' said Charles irritably. 'Stands to reason.'

Hangover, deduced Penny.

The bride reached for a fourth piece of toast and covered it lavishly with butter and marmalade.

'Don't fuss, Mummy. If the worst comes to the worst Penny can make me up a bouquet from the garden.'

'Thank you for your vote of confidence,' Penny said drily.

Celia gave her a most unmodel-like grin. 'Do you remember those presentation bouquets we used to make for Daddy?'

Penny gave a startled chuckle. 'Nettles and bindweed, you mean? You want to walk down the aisle carrying stuff salvaged from the compost heap?'

'Well, bindweed is pretty,' Celia said in a judicial tone. At her mother's look of horror, she collapsed in giggles.

'She doesn't mean it,' Penny said soothingly as Laura began to get to her feet in protest.

Charles grinned. 'You're naughty girls, winding your mother up like that.' He said to Zoltan in explanation, 'When they were small, I was up for one of the European awards where they gave you flowers—men and women alike. The girls overheard me talking about it to Laura and decided to help out.' His voice was warm with reminiscence. 'They staged presentation ceremonies every night after school. They weren't allowed to pick flowers from the garden, of course, so they had to use weeds. They took it in turns to receive the award but as far as I can remember it was always Penny who made up the bouquets.'

'An artist even then?' asked Zoltan teasingly.

There was a warmth in his eyes which made Penny glad that there was someone to answer for her.

Celia nodded. 'She was the only one who was any good at it. Leslie's and mine fell apart and Angel put stinging-nettles in hers which brought everyone out in a rash.'

'No stinging-nettles,' Penny murmured, as one making a note.

'I think I'll just go and ring the florist again,' Laura said, rising.

She hurried out. Charles picked up his paper. Celia laughed. She was so happy she shone, Penny thought.

'Poor Mummy. It will come out all right. It has to on a wonderful day like this,' she said buoyantly. 'Is there any more coffee, Pen?'

'Good lord,' said Charles, reading, '"Wife of twenty years gets injunction against husband." You'd think it wouldn't take her twenty years to notice the man beat her up.' He looked round the edge of the paper. 'Yes, thank you, darling, I'll have some too.'

Penny stiffened slightly. Zoltan saw it. She realised it too late, as his eyes narrowed across the table at her. Another betrayal of her private feelings. Why did he have to notice? Nobody else had. Damn, damn, damn.

She got up. 'The pot is cold. I'll make some more.'

She went to the cupboard. She could feel his eyes on her—thoughtful, assessing. *Damn*.

Celia said dreamily, 'Today is the start of the rest of my life.'

'Yes, poppet,' said Charles. 'Not that it's exactly a revolution. You've been living with the man for long enough.'

Celia was unabashed. 'We wanted to be sure before we made a commitment.'

Charles shook his head, clearly only half convinced.

'Well, at least you know he won't beat you, I suppose,' He shook the paper. 'Did you read this? I don't know why your mother thinks Hollywood is such a den of iniquity. It seems to me it all happens in the Home Counties. This woman claims her husband beat her up twice a week for twenty years. If it took her twenty years to leave him then she must have liked it.'

Penny felt her skin go cold, as it had in the long-ago past. She kept her back turned to them and switched on the coffee grinder. It was too loud to make an answer possible.

'Ouch,' said Charles, when the noise died away. 'That's not a thing to do to a man with a hangover, darling.'

'If you had an ounce of decent feeling you wouldn't have a hangover,' Penny said lightly, not turning round.

She found filter papers and tipped the coffee competently into one. She measured water into the glass tank, reconstructed the machine and switched it on.

Charles assumed his noblest voice. 'A man's entitled to get drunk when he gives away his last little girl,' he said.

Celia crowed with laughter. Penny gasped and turned round in spite of herself. She caught Zoltan's eye at once. There was a question there, but it was also brimful of laughter. Suddenly her own lips twitched. She sat down on one of the kitchen chairs, shaking her head.

'Charles, you are outrageous,' she said frankly. 'None of us has been your little girl for fifteen years.'

But Charles was enjoying playing the regretful father. 'Do you remember your wedding, Pen? I was so nervous I lost your bouquet. And your mother cried through the whole thing.' He sighed reminiscently.

Penny winced. All desire to laugh left her abruptly. What could she say? *You weren't nervous, you were furious. You didn't want me to marry him. That's why Mother cried too. And you were both right.*

No, that wasn't a possibility. For one thing, you didn't talk about your own marital disasters at someone else's wedding. For another, her family didn't know exactly what a disaster it had been. It had become a matter of pride to keep it from them in the end.

'I remember,' she said without expression.

Celia shuddered. 'Don't talk about losing bouquets. I'm not superstitious but there's no need to go looking for bad luck.'

Zoltan leaned forward to Penny. 'You were married from this house too?'

Penny did not answer. But Charles was only too willing to do so for her.

'It wasn't like this,' he assured him with a grimace. 'Pen was still a student. She never liked frills anyway. It was just a family party.'

'A student?' Zoltan was frowning slightly, as if the news surprised him. 'So young?' His eyes narrowed suddenly, as if he'd remembered a crucial clue in a game of wits. 'Nineteen?' he asked softly.

Double damn. She should never have told him that. Penny nodded briefly, not allowing him to meet her eyes.

'Pen always knows her own mind,' Charles said. There was a faintly defensive note in his voice.

And rushes headlong to disaster following it, Penny thought wryly. She did not say it, though. Her father knew that her marriage had been as big a mistake as he had predicted. Fortunately he did not know exactly how big a mistake. There was no need for Zoltan Guard to know anything at all.

The coffee was ready. The kitchen was full of the comforting aroma. She got up and brought the jug to the table.

Her father held out his cup. Celia pushed his newspaper out of the way. Her eye fell on the article.

'You know, it is odd,' she said, with the confidence of one possessing a sunny nature and a devoted lover. 'I mean, why didn't she leave him if he beat her up?'

Penny's hand shook a little. She steadied the coffee pot and poured carefully into her father's cup.

'Maybe she didn't have anywhere else to go,' she said levelly.

'But there are refuges,' Celia said, puzzled.

'Maybe she was afraid.' Penny pushed the cup towards her father, gave some to Celia and at last, reluctantly, looked at Zoltan. 'More coffee?'

The eyes were frighteningly acute as he passed his cup across to her.

She took it, looking quickly at Celia and her father. But no, knowing her well, they still detected nothing. Oh, if only she had not been so indiscreet last night. If only she had *thought*, instead of allowing herself to be swept away by the strangeness of it all. If only she had not given Zoltan so many clues.

'It is easy to be afraid when you are in a violent relationship,' Zoltan said, his eyes on her face.

Penny studied the stream of coffee as she poured. She could feel his gaze on her face like a heat-lamp, she thought in confusion.

'I suppose so,' she said colourlessly.

Charles snorted again. 'Violent relationships! Psychobabble. If a man hits a woman then any woman worth her salt walks out on him the first time he does it. If she doesn't, she's just asking for more,' he announced.

Penny felt as if he had tipped ice water over her. She felt her spine freeze, her whole flesh and nerves turn to ice in one juddering moment of shock. Her hand shook. Hastily she put the coffee-pot down, heedless for once of whether it marked the wooden table. She could feel the blood leaving her face.

Zoltan leaned forward and took the cup away from her.

'You'd think so, certainly,' he said easily.

He stood up and went to the window so that her father had to shift slightly to carry on talking to him. He leaned against the worktop, cradling the coffee in front of him. He looked, she thought suddenly, as if he were conducting a seminar. For the first time she could see him as an academic.

'But it is extraordinary what the human animal can get used to. Convince itself is normal, even.' His voice was dispassionate. 'There is a basic tendency to inertia,

GET 4 BOOKS A FLUFFY DUCK AND A MYSTERY GIFT

FREE

Return this card, and we'll send you 4 specially selected Mills & Boon romances absolutely FREE! We'll even pay the postage and packing for you!

We're making this offer to introduce you to the benefits of Reader Service: FREE home delivery of brand-new romances at least a month before they're available in the shops, FREE gifts and a monthly Newsletter packed with information.

Accepting these FREE books places you under no obligation to buy, you may cancel at any time simply by writing to us — even after receiving just your free shipment.

← TEAR OFF AND POST THIS CARD TODAY ←

Yes, please send me 4 free Mills & Boon romances, a fluffy duck and a mystery gift. I understand that unless you hear from me, I will receive 6 superb new titles every month for just £1.99* each postage and packing free. I am under no obligation to purchase any books and I may cancel or suspend my subscription at any time, but the free books and gifts will be mine to keep in any case.

(I am over 18 years of age).

4A5R

Ms/Mrs/Miss/Mr _____

Address _____

_____

_____ Postcode _____

*Prices subject to change without notice.

Get 4 books
a fluffy duck and
mystery gift FREE!

SEE OVER FOR DETAILS

Harlequin Mills & Boon
FREEPOST
P. O. Box 70
Croydon
Surrey
CR9 9EL

Offer closes 31st October 1995. We reserve the right to refuse an application. *Prices and terms subject to change without notice. Offer valid in U.K. and Eire only and is not available to current subscribers of this series. Overseas readers please write for details. Southern Africa write to: IBS Private Bag X3010, Randburg 2125.

You may be mailed with offers from other reputable companies as a result of this application. If you would prefer not to share in this opportunity, please tick box. ☐

of course. Psychologically speaking, the individual fears that any change in one's circumstances will be for the worse.' He chuckled suddenly. 'Michael told me that the English call it Murphy's Law—anything that can go wrong will. And then unprecedented action is particularly difficult for an individual. Groups reinforce each other—whether they are football fans or rocket scientists—but the isolated individual takes on the whole world. And there are few people as isolated as the woman in a violent marriage. One can understand how it happens.'

The words flowed over her—measured, unemotional. Penny drew steadying breaths, pressing her hands together out of sight of her father. Slowly she could feel the blood begin to flow again. She poured herself coffee and gulped it down.

Her father shrugged. He looked unconvinced. 'You may be right. I've never known anyone like that.'

Oh, haven't you? thought Penny with wincing irony. Did I do such a wonderful job of disguising it? Or did you just not want to see?

Celia said compassionately, 'Poor things. It must be awful not to have a family to back you up.' She reached out across the tablecloth and squeezed Penny's hand affectionately. 'If it were me, I'd run to my big sister.'

Penny smiled but it was an effort. Oh, no, you wouldn't, she thought sadly. You're too like me. You'd keep it quiet and hope it would change and not tell a soul.

She said impulsively, 'Be happy, Cilly.'

Celia smiled. 'I will. I am.' She added mischievously, 'Even if we have to raid the compost heap for my bouquet.'

Charles said, 'Well, your mother won't be. Go and find out if she's spoken to the wretched florist yet, will you, love?'

Celia went obligingly. As soon as she'd gone, he leaned forward.

'Can you really make up some sort of bouquet for her, Pen? If there's been a hitch, I mean?'

Penny said doubtfully, 'Not out of the garden. There's not enough in flower. Well, maybe something for Celia but not the bridesmaids as well. And that big urn in the drawing-room will take some filling.'

Zoltan moved. He said lazily, 'Is there anything stopping you going out to buy more flowers locally?'

Penny jumped. 'I suppose not,' she said slowly.

'Brilliant,' said Charles enthusiastically. 'Take someone with you. There'll be a lot to carry.' He looked meaningly at their guest.

Zoltan looked amused. 'I was just about to offer.'

'There's no need,' Penny said stiffly.

'Yes, there is. You said it yourself. That damn great urn takes half a tree to fill it up. In fact you'd better take the estate car and load the stuff in the back.'

Penny hesitated. She did not like driving the estate car which was a great deal longer and heavier than her own runabout.

Charles, who was well aware of her prejudice, beamed.

'Zoltan can drive,' he said with apparent inspiration.

Zoltan's amusement deepened. 'Delighted,' he said.

There was nothing she could do, Penny realised. It was perfectly obvious that they were being manoeuvred. It was also obvious that Zoltan thought it was funny— and she was not going to be able to avoid it without being rude or so elaborately evasive as to invite questions. Neither of which would do anything to add to the happiness of Celia's day.

'Thank you,' she said with restraint.

He tilted his head, laughing down at her. 'Any time.'

She looked at her watch. 'If I'm going to do it, we'd better get going.'

Charles nodded. 'Do that. Not a word to Laura.'

Penny looked surprised.

'I'm going to hold the line that professional florists don't let their customers down,' he said. 'Then she won't start to panic until you've got some more flowers back here.' He pulled out his wallet and rummaged through it. 'You don't want dollars. What—oh, yes, here it is. I cashed a cheque yesterday. Take that. It probably won't be enough so——'

'I can put any excess on my credit card,' Penny assured him.

'Thank God for plastic.' Charles grinned. 'I never thought I'd live to hear myself say that.'

On the kitchen wall, the telephone began to ring. He went to answer it, fishing a set of car keys off the hook in the memory board beside it.

'Hello. Oh, hello, Jonas. Lost your map?' He tossed the keys to Zoltan, who caught them one-handed. 'Yes, of course I can tell you how to get to the church. Got to get there myself, haven't I?' He waved them out of the kitchen, saying into the telephone, 'Got a pencil...?'

'Coming?' Zoltan was at the kitchen door.

Penny went, hoping her reluctance didn't show.

'Don't look so worried,' he said, knocking that one on the head as soon as they were out of the door. 'I promise not to jump on you in the back of the car.'

'Don't be ridiculous,' she said, leading the way to the garage. 'It never occurred to me that you would.'

'Then you don't know anything about Californian courting habits,' he said blandly. 'When I was growing up it was standard behaviour.'

'One would have hoped you had grown up by now, however,' she pointed out acidly.

He laughed. 'Some things you never forget.'

She unlocked the garage door. 'Well, try,' she advised him. 'We haven't got time for silly games.'

'Especially as you don't play games,' he agreed.

Penny looked at him sharply but his face stayed bland. He followed her into the garage and identified the car without difficulty. It was wedged tightly between Celia's open-topped cabriolet and her mother's car. Neither was well parked.

'I'll get the keys and move one of those,' Penny said.

'No need.'

Zoltan vaulted lightly over Celia's car and opened the door of the estate. It was the narrowest possible gap but he eased himself through it, holding his ribcage in and laughing. He drove the car out into the sun without adding a mark to any of the closely packed cars. For some reason the lazy expertise annoyed Penny.

'Very proficient,' she said, getting into the passenger seat and closing the door unnecessarily hard.

'The word,' Zoltan told her drily, 'is professional. While I was in college I parked cars for a living.'

He let in the clutch and they were away.

'You parked cars in Hungary?' said Penny, boggling at this unlikely scenario. 'Where?'

He laughed. 'No. No. California. My father would not have allowed me to soil my hands with automobiles when I was at home. I was supposed to be a boy genius.'

'Oh, I see. Did you do an exchange with an American university?'

'No.' He was cool. 'I emigrated. When I was fourteen.'

She was surprised. 'So long ago? That shows how little one knows about the rest of the world. I always assumed it wasn't permitted.'

He smiled. 'It wasn't.'

'What?'

'I was a political refugee,' he explained. 'I went over the border at dead of night, expecting to be caught at any moment.'

She said, 'But you can't have been a political refugee at fourteen. It's—you were a *child*, for heaven's sake.'

Zoltan looked down at her. 'I was never a child.'

'*What?*'

He shrugged. 'I was the only son of a man who had once been a genius. He didn't hold with childhood. And unfortunately the system supported him.' They turned on to the main road. 'Where now?'

'Right at the crossroads.' She was struggling to digest the information. None of it made sense. 'What do you mean? How can he have been a genius once? Geniuses don't go off,' she protested.

He sent her a quick look. 'They do if they're mathematicians. I've always been grateful I wasn't only a mathematician. There's probably some chemical reason for it. Most mathematicians have done their best work by the time they're thirty. Earlier, even. At twenty-five my father had worldwide acclaim. He was reading papers all over the world. At forty he was forgotten.'

Penny's eyes narrowed. 'Are you saying you were his second chance?'

His eyebrows rose. 'Clever,' he approved. 'Something like that, certainly.'

She shook her head. 'What happened?'

'Nothing very terrible. I was gifted. Extraordinarily gifted. So I was taken away from my parents and sent to school with my peers. All over the Soviet Union at one time or another. I only went back to Hungary when I was thirteen.'

Penny thought of her own disorderly childhood. The schools had changed but there had always been one or the other of her parents and her sisters.

She said, 'That's terrible.'

'That's what I thought,' Zoltan agreed. 'I blamed the Communist regime, of course. I swore I would get out and lead my own life as soon as I could. It was a terrible shock when I got to the West to find that gifted children aren't treated so different here. Although I was older then. Getting to see that human nature isn't so different, no matter what the political organisation. But it was still a shock. In fact,' he added thoughtfully, 'that was probably my last illusion.'

Penny had a crazy urge to apologise to him for the loss of that illusion. She even opened her lips to speak. Then she looked at him, tall and powerfully compact, with laughing eyes and that devil-may-care tilt to his head, and thought better of it. This was not a man who needed sympathy from anyone.

As if he were reading her mind, he said, 'I've done just fine without illusions. Although I suppose there was one that was not so great to lose.' He did not take his eyes off the windscreen this time. 'That love-affair you were asking about last night.'

Penny blushed. 'I wasn't. I——'

'Yes, you were. Quite rightly.'

'I had no right——' she began uncomfortably.

'You had every right if you wanted to know.' Zoltan drove carefully round a blind corner. 'Do you?'

Penny stared at the road with concentration. She had met him less than twenty-four hours ago. He had laughed at her and ordered her around and nearly taken her into some very dangerous territory indeed last night. He also seemed to know exactly whenever something was important to her, no matter how carefully she monitored her reactions or how obliquely she spoke. And she knew nothing at all about him. She made up her mind.

'Yes,' she said.

'It was a long time ago,' he said evenly. 'I was young. Though not as young as nineteen. She was everything a young man dreams about, I suppose—beautiful, beautifully brought up, clever, well-connected.' He checked their speed over a hump-backed bridge. 'On reflection I think I was probably as much in love with her family as I was with her. They were all clever and they lived in this wonderful house in New Hampshire.' He looked sideways at her. 'Not unlike yours in some ways.'

Did that account for the reserve she sensed in him? The slight air of mystery which he had shown no desire to dispel?

'Do we remind you?' she asked tentatively.

'In some ways. Not all. They were a very competitive family. You—well, you have your differences but you look after each other. I can see that now. They just wanted to beat each other. Katherine most of all.'

'I see,' said Penny. 'Did she want to beat you too?'

He smiled. It was a mirthless twist of the lips.

'Yes and no. Yes, she wanted to win; she was ferocious if she didn't. No, she didn't want to live with a man who was beaten by anyone—even herself.'

'It sounds like hell,' Penny said involuntarily.

'It had its moments,' he admitted.

'Were you married?'

'That was the only stupidity I didn't commit. She wanted to. But I—wasn't sure. It went on too long, though, while we battled it out. In the end she said it was my fault it hadn't worked. And in part she had to be right. But she was hyper-competitive before she met me and it's gone on since. I'm told she's on her third husband now.'

Something in his tone made her look at him.

'Still carrying a torch, Zoltan?'

He shrugged. 'No. The burn-marks, maybe. It taught me hard but it taught me well. No permanent relationships.'

'I see,' said Penny again.

And she did. Rather too clearly for her own peace of mind. After all, what was it to her if Zoltan Guard was not going to consider permanent commitment? She barely knew the man. And yet it hurt, somewhere secret and deeply private; it hurt rather a lot.

'She's a main board director of the family bank now. That was what she wanted me to do, of course. Said there was no future in the academic life. She'd have hated

it if I'd got to the board before she did, too. Anyway,
that wasn't for me.' His voice grew amused suddenly.
'In fact I did a consultancy project for them last year.
It was a bit small for me really, but I thought I owed
her old man. He was good to me in his way. Even lent
me money once.'

She said, 'Do academics do consultancies for banks?'
although she was not in the least bit interested. She was
only interested in keeping his eyes off her until this fierce
little pain died down.

'All the time. I'm much in demand.' He laughed. 'So
much that I name my own price these days.'

She gave a sudden choke of laughter. 'And my mother
thought you were a starving academic who could do with
a square meal.'

'Last night I was.' He sent her another of those quick
looks. 'In all sorts of ways.'

'Yes, well. Turn left at the next roundabout,' Penny
said uncomfortably. 'It's not much more than a village
but they might have some flowers here. Through the
traffic lights, and it's the second parade of shops.'

He followed her instructions. She leapt out, expecting
him to wait for her in the car. But he got out and strolled
into the shop after her.

'You get flowers here?' he said, looking round at the
racks of local organic vegetables.

'Well, I'm not sending my sister down the aisle
clutching a cauliflower,' snapped Penny, unaccountably
disturbed by his warm presence at her shoulder.

He laughed. 'From what I saw this morning, I
wouldn't think she'd care.'

'My mother would,' Penny said unanswerably.

The shopkeeper came out to greet them. Penny
explained the problem. The shopkeeper shook her head.

'I get my flowers from Meadowbanks fresh every day,'
she explained. 'I'm on my own this morning so I didn't
go over.'

Penny's heart dropped to her toes. She looked at her watch.

'Maybe there's time to get to Shrewsbury if you put your foot down,' she said.

Zoltan did not move from the spot. He smiled at the shopkeeper lazily.

'How about if we went to Meadowbanks?' he asked.

The woman looked doubtful. 'Well, they really only sell wholesale.'

'That's no problem. The lady's father says we need the equivalent of half a tree,' he said with a grin.

She smiled back. The famous charm working again, Penny thought sourly. She danced with impatience.

'No—I mean just to trade,' amended the shopkeeper.

'Come *on*,' said Penny. 'We're wasting time.'

'But if we were collecting flowers for you we would be buying for the trade, wouldn't we?' he suggested.

The shopkeeper nodded slowly. 'I suppose I could give you my card. They know me, of course, but...'

'You call them and say you're on your own and can't get out there but neighbours are picking up your order,' said Zoltan fluently. His grin widened. 'It's even true.'

The shopkeeper nodded. 'I could do that.'

'Fine. Then all we need is a list of whatever you want. Do you pay Meadowbanks cash or put it on account?'

Penny watched in deep dudgeon as he and the woman organised the mechanics of paying for the flowers. From the slightly bemused expression on the woman's face she guessed that he was either offering her particularly generous terms for the flowers or was overwhelming her with that charm.

'I suppose you think you're very clever,' she said when they were back in the car.

One eyebrow flicked up. 'Angry with me?' he sounded amused and not very surprised.

'I don't like the way you order everyone around for your own convenience.'

'On this occasion for your convenience,' he pointed out. 'And I don't order. I just smooth the path to help people to do what I want. Just show them it's what they want to do too, really.'

Out of nowhere came his voice from last night. 'It was an offer, not a command.' Penny flushed brilliant scarlet. I wish I would stop doing that, she thought furiously.

'Oh, is that what it is? Well, you're suspiciously good at it.'

'I ought to be,' he said calmly. 'It's my job. Well, the well-paid bit of my job anyway.'

'*What*?'

He looked down at her, his eyes dancing. 'You, my dear girl, have just had the benefit of several thousand dollars' worth of management advice. Implementation thrown in, too. I shouldn't be too rude about it if I were you. My clients wouldn't like to hear I'm giving it away for free.'

They collected the flowers, along with the shop-keeper's order. Penny was allowed to go out into the gardens to choose her own flowers. She did so, her eyes daring Zoltan to go with her. He laughed, shrugged, and stayed in the run-down office.

Back on the road to the manor, the back of the car piled with flowers and greenery, Zoltan said idly, 'Why didn't you have this sort of wedding as well? When you were nineteen and so in love?'

Penny lifted her head, surprised.

'Your father mentioned it at breakfast,' he reminded her.

'Oh. Yes.' She smiled. Choosing the flowers had exercised a calming effect on her temper. 'Partly it's not my style. Partly—— Well, you may as well know. My family weren't ecstatic about my marriage anyway.'

He nodded as if it was what he had expected. 'I bet you were stunning at nineteen,' he said softly. 'Stunning, head over heels in love, disapproving parents. I bet you weren't even pregnant.'

Between astonishment and outrage, Penny gave a choke of shocked laughter. 'How do you know that?'

'Because you gambled all your emotional resources on one man,' he said slowly. 'If there had been a child you wouldn't have been able to. You would have had to keep something back for the baby.'

Penny was silenced. 'You're too clever,' she said at last with a little shiver.

'I'm interested,' he said, not denying it. 'Tell me about your husband. What happened to him?'

She looked out of the window. The sun had come out and made the surface of the road gleam as if it were melting. She could face it as long as told him just the bare facts.

'He died,' she said. 'Two years ago. He was killed in an accident.'

It was the truth but not the whole truth. She wondered if he would notice the evasion. He did.

'And that's all you're going to tell me.' He did not sound annoyed about it. 'Well, leave it for the moment. Tell me instead how you met. Was he as young as you?'

Fact again. She could handle facts. Penny shrugged. 'No. He was a painter. He borrowed a studio down here for the summer. I was at art college. He gave me lessons. We fell in love. We married. End of story.'

'I usually think of marriage as the beginning of the story rather than the end,' Zoltan said.

'That,' muttered Penny to the passing road, 'depends on the story.'

She did not say it loudly. She did not expect him to hear. But of course he did. He reached out a hand and covered her own.

'One day you will tell me,' he said. It sounded like a vow. 'One day you will tell me the whole story.'

CHAPTER SIX

FORTUNATELY he was not able to demand any more revelations because at that moment the manor's entrance came into view. Penny drew a sigh of relief.

None of the family was anywhere to be seen but the ladies from the Women's Institute reported that Mrs Brinkman was very agitated—and the flowers had still not arrived. Penny went into the kitchen and set about finding the wherewithal to make bouquets. Before she had even begun to look the Women's Institute produced stiffened wire, secateurs, and other refinements she had never even imagined when producing her earlier creations.

Zoltan, to the expressed admiration of the entire Women's Institute party, carried in boxes of flowers without complaint. Penny suspected darkly that it was his charm at work again which won her three volunteers to help with bridesmaids' bouquets.

Whether it was or not, she was grateful. The whole business took much longer than she had expected. Finally she dressed the big urn in the drawing-room in fifteen minutes flat.

Leaving one of her kind helpers to trail leaves artistically, she took the stairs at a run. Zoltan, holding the urn, flashed her a wicked, intimate smile. As one, the Women's Institute sighed. Breathing hard, Penny flung into her room and dragged her new outfit from the wardrobe. In the act of doing so, she caught sight of herself in the long mirror on the back of the old-fashioned door to the wardrobe. She stopped, arrested.

For the first time in months she surveyed herself. It was a pleasant enough image that met her eyes, she allowed dispassionately. Undistinguished, but there was nothing absolutely ugly about it. Tall—above the average. Probably too thin but that was fashionable and she did not worry about it. In the years with Alan she had gone from worrying about youthful plumpness to concern that her skeletal condition would cause comment. Now she was just grateful to be back within the average range and seldom thought about her figure. In comparison with the voluptuous Celia, though, there was no doubt that she looked like a beanpole, she thought now.

Penny felt the first stirrings of dissatisfaction with her appearance that she had felt for years. She put her hands on her hips and squared up to it. Her chin lifted a little.

The smart new haircut had left a cluster of curls clinging to the soft curve of her neck, accentuating the graceful length. It also made her look absurdly young and vulnerable, Penny saw now, with a little shock of displeasure.

'I am not vulnerable,' she told her image grimly.

The mirror image looked back at her, disproving her claim. Her eyes looked enormous under the level brows. They had gone the colour of her jade pendant. They always did that when she was on edge, she thought disgustedly. It was one of the ways Alan had been able to tell when she was most vulnerable...

She caught herself. She was not going to think about Alan. She was not going to do any more remembering today. Marriage was in the past; she had dealt with it and, as she had told Sue Flynn, she knew its price. She was not in the market for another relationship, especially not some fleeting, volatile exchange with a man she did not understand—who seemed to understand her all too well.

She thought of his fingers at the back of her neck last night and shivered again. All too well in all sorts of ways.

She turned away from the mirror. What was happening to her? You would almost think she was in love with the man, the way she kept referring back to incidents much better forgotten. Keep a hold of yourself, she thought. After this weekend is over you aren't going to see him again.

She shivered for the third time. It was the safest thing, she told herself. She should be grateful that she could say an uncomplicated goodbye to him before she got too involved. But she could not quite banish the oddly forlorn feeling it gave her.

'Stupid,' Penny told herself aloud, fiercely.

She stripped off her jeans and loose sweater without once looking back in the mirror and went to run her bath. After a soak in the scented water she felt steadier. She slipped on her old towelling robe and padded out into her bedroom to fetch fresh underwear.

There was a knock at the door. Bent over her weekend case, Penny froze momentarily. He wouldn't, she thought. He *wouldn't*. Not in a house full of people, any one of whom might see him and draw the right conclusions. Not when they would all be gathering in the local church in an hour and he would have to look her family in the eye.

Oh, but he would, another part of her mind thought. He was the only man she had ever met who was really, deeply indifferent to what people thought of him. Even Alan at his wildest had still cared about other people's good opinion. But not Zoltan. He would probably not even notice, Penny thought.

Her lips twitched and she straightened. She would have to send him away, of course. But she liked that indifference to public opinion. It was one of the things she found most attractive about him, she thought unguardedly.

'Careful,' she muttered, catching herself.

She tightened the towelling belt and opened the door. 'This is not very sensible——' she began. And stopped.

It was not Zoltan. It was Celia. Her sister was wearing a silky kimono pulled untidily over a froth of white underwear and a long hooped petticoat. Her hair was piled high and she had a veil and a pretty coronet of fresh flowers in the blonde silkiness. She had lost her earlier luminous glow. Her expression was closer to panic.

'Come in,' Penny said, concerned.

Celia nodded. She was trembling slightly. Penny saw the way the much-photographed lips shook. She slid an arm round Celia's shoulders.

'Sit down,' she said practically. 'What's wrong?'

'Mummy.' Celia's normal guileless blue eyes were shadowed with distress.

'Ah,' said Penny.

'She's been in my room going on and on and on...'

So that was why there had been no members of the family around when they got back. She poured her sister a glass of mineral water from the bottle on her bedside table and put it into her hand.

'Calm down, love. I take it the flowers didn't arrive?'

'No. The van broke down on the motorway. How did you——?'

Penny told her about Charles' rescue plan. 'When we got back and the Women's Institute said the flowers hadn't arrived, I just sat down and did you a bouquet,' she said. 'I should have come and told you—but to be honest, Cilly, I just went at it hammer and tongs because of the time.'

She cast a surreptitious look at her watch. Celia didn't notice. She was too busy bursting into grateful tears.

'I told her you'd do something. I *told* her. But she kept saying there weren't enough flowers in the garden and I'd have to carry a hymn book or something and it was all Daddy's fault.' Celia sniffed. 'Why didn't Daddy say?'

Penny thought privately that Charles had probably got too annoyed at her mother's reproaches. He had a notoriously short fuse and he was not very happy about having his home turned upside-down, even for a beloved daughter's wedding.

But she said diplomatically, 'He probably thought he'd better not until he found out whether we'd managed to find any flowers in time.'

Celia raised eyes like drowned cornflowers.

'We?'

'Charles sent Zoltan Guard with me as chauffeur-cum-native bearer,' said Penny briefly.

'Oh.'

A small complacent smile flickered briefly across her sister's lovely face. It disappeared so quickly that Penny could not even be certain she had seen it. I am getting paranoid, she told herself.

'He's nice, isn't he?' Celia said airily.

'He's an opinionated, devious man with a nasty habit of amusing himself at other people's expense,' Penny said roundly.

Celia blinked. 'I thought he was rather glamorous,' she said in a small voice.

'Oh, he's that as well,' Penny said bitterly. 'No doubt he's given you a burst of the world-famous charm?'

'*What*?'

'His description, not mine.'

Celia giggled. 'Mike says every woman thinks he's a knock-out,' she said in congratulatory tones.

Penny's eyes narrowed.

'In that case,' she said with dangerous quiet, 'why did you send me to the station looking for Albert Einstein last night?'

Celia took a hasty sip of water which turned into a prolonged coughing fit. When Penny had thumped her none too gently on the back she got her breath and denied ever doing any such thing.

'Anyway, I didn't know what he would be like. I've never met him until today. I don't trust Mike's opinion, after all. Men are never reliable about other men, are they?' Celia said, desperately trying to retrieve the situation.

She was not successful. Penny looked at her broodingly.

'You set me up.'

Celia gave her a dazzling but tentative smile. 'Only a little. Honestly, Pen, I just wanted you to have a nice time. It seemed so miserable all the rest of us being happy and having our men to hold our hands and you not having anyone. I sort of couldn't bear it. Not on my wedding-day.'

Penny shook her head. 'The trouble with you is you're a hopeless romantic. Didn't it occur to you I might not *want* anyone?'

Celia dismissed that as frivolous. 'Pride gets you no-where,' she said sagely. 'You wanted someone once.'

Penny winced. Celia looked intrigued. She was staring at her sister unblinkingly. The tears seemed to have subsided.

'What did go wrong for you, Pen?' she asked.

Penny bit her lip.

'Lots of things. It was wrong from the start. We just didn't know enough about each other.'

'And you couldn't find out after you were married?' Celia sounded disappointed, just like the little sister who had cried herself to sleep complaining that Fanny Price had married the wrong man. 'He was so gorgeous. I remember when you got married—I envied you so much. I thought, I'll never find a man as lovely as that. And you seemed so in love.' Her eyes grew misty again.

'Infatuated is the word,' Penny said sharply.

Celia looked at her wonderingly. 'Would you have got back together again? If he hadn't died like that, I mean.'

'No.' It was uncompromising.

Celia was disappointed again. 'But he adored you. I remember the way he used to look at you. Sort of smouldering.' She gave a little wriggle. 'It used to make my insides melt just to see it.'

Penny remembered that look too. Even across the years it still had the power to make her throat close and the palms of her hands sweat. Because, unlike Celia, she knew what came after.

'We were divorced,' she said levelly. 'I didn't do that lightly. I considered very carefully whether I could go back to him before ever I petitioned for divorce. I couldn't. The marriage was over.'

It should never have begun, of course. But you didn't say that to your sister on her wedding-day. In spite of her restraint her sister looked a little alarmed.

'Oh, God, what if something like that happened to Mike and me? I couldn't bear it without Mike. I really couldn't. He can hurt me so easily. I know I ought not to let him. That it's weak and silly and I ought to be ashamed of myself. But I can't help it.'

Tears seemed to threaten again. This wedding, Penny thought with resignation, was going to deplete her emotional reserves for the next fifty years one way and another. Oh, for the peace of the office and the bellowing of offended consultants! She applied herself to soothing her sister's nerves.

She said gently. 'You and Michael are different people from Alan and me. It isn't as if you don't know each other. You've lived together for over a year. You talk. You trust each other. That's why you're getting married. It's silly to say you mustn't let him hurt you. If you love each other, of course you can hurt each other. It's part of the deal. You can't say, I'll marry you but only a bit, and then I'll be safe from being hurt. It doesn't work like that.'

Celia stared at her.

'Alan hurt you,' she said slowly, on a note of discovery.

Penny did not blink. 'Divorce is a nasty business. I've no doubt I hurt him too. Look, this is a crazy conversation for your wedding-day.' She hugged her sister. 'You're in love with Mike. The sun is shining. And you don't even have to walk up the aisle carrying a cauliflower,' she added irrepressibly.

Celia looked startled. 'A cauliflower?'

'We got the flowers from the greengrocer's in the village.'

Celia grinned. 'That would have made a nice feature in the family album.'

'Well, you can forget it. You've got a bouquet of camellias and maidenhair fern with a few grape hyacinths thrown in for something blue,' Penny said. She turned her hands over for inspection. 'I've scratched myself all over with that blasted chicken-wire doing it, too. So if you don't carry it I shall personally strangle you.'

'You'd be in the queue after Mummy,' Celia said, undisturbed by the threat. She stood up and kissed Penny's cheek. 'You're the best sister in the world, Pen.' She sighed. 'I just wish there was someone nice for you.'

'Wish all you like but don't do anything about it,' Penny said firmly. 'Please.'

'What?'

'I'm told it's a syndrome called the wedding effect. My friends have been warning me about it. The urge for one successful wedding to spawn another,' Penny explained. 'Matchmaking between unmarried parties present. Largely undertaken by the bride and her mother, I understand,' she added darkly.

Celia giggled again.

'I wouldn't dare. And after today Mummy will probably pay you not to marry again,' she said cheerfully. 'She was going to lie down on her bed with cologne-soaked pads on her eyelids when last seen.' She grinned. 'So you're quite safe.'

Penny thought of the man who had been dominating her thoughts for the last twenty-four hours. *Safe*? She was shaken by a little laugh. Celia watched her from under exquisite eyelashes.

'Unless the gorgeous prof makes a play for you off his own bat, of course.'

Penny blushed faintly. 'Don't be ridiculous.'

'Why is it ridiculous? He was asking all sorts of things about you this morning. I'd say he was distinctly interested.'

'Oh, *interested*.' Penny laughed dismissively. 'Yes, I'll give you that. He kept saying last night how interesting I was.'

'Well, you are,' Celia said stoutly. 'Especially as you seem to have been frightfully brave about the burglars. I gather we aren't telling Mummy in case she has the heebie-jeebies. But Zoltan was telling Daddy you were an absolute heroine through it all.'

Penny blushed deeper. 'Exaggeration,' she said gruffly.

'Zoltan didn't seem to think so.' Celia examined her nails. 'Honestly, Pen, I think he's really smitten.'

'You're letting the romance of the wedding go to your head,' Penny said drily. 'That man has never been seriously smitten in the whole of his life.' And as her sister looked disbelieving she added in a goaded voice, 'He *told* me he didn't believe in permanence.'

'Permanent what?' asked Celia innocently.

Penny shot her a cool look. 'As I recall, he was discussing drowning in my eyes at the time. Quite temporarily, as he pointed out.'

Celia gave a crow of laughter. 'How wonderful. In that case I think you might just as well start writing out your formal surrender now.'

'Surrender? You're talking nonsense. Why on earth should I?'

'Because I don't see any red-blooded woman resisting Zoltan Guard,' Celia said simply. 'Not for long, anyway.'

'He won't be here for long,' Penny said.

But she was disconcerted. And just a little uneasy.

If she was aware of it then Celia was shrewd enough not to say any more. She swallowed the last of the mineral water.

'I suppose you haven't got a real drink?' she said wistfully. 'I could really do with a glass of champagne.'

'Wait for it,' Penny advised. 'The place will be awash with the stuff in a couple of hours.'

There was another knock on the door.

'This is like Paddington station,' she muttered, going to open it.

Celia helped herself to a tissue and blew her nose loudly.

'No, it isn't. You can get a drink on Paddington station,' she said with a grin. Her equilibrium seemed fully restored. 'Who...? Oh,' she ended on a long note of surprise. She sent her sister a mischievous look.

Penny was speechless. All she could think was, He did dare. I should have known. Silently she stood aside to admit her visitor. Her hands went quickly to check the tie of her old robe. She tightened it anyway.

Zoltan Guard gave them both an impartial flash of that dazzling smile and strolled into her room. Suddenly it seemed smaller.

'Funny you should mention that,' he said. 'I was thinking along the same lines myself.' He produced a silver-topped bottle and began to strip away the foil in a businesslike fashion.

Celia gave a long sigh. 'Champagne,' she said dreamily.

'Inspired,' Penny said, with something of a snap. 'Celia was just demanding it.'

His quick glance said he noted her flicker of annoyance. From the way his mouth just tilted, very slightly, Penny concluded that it amused him. She tugged her towelling sash even tighter and glared at him.

He withstood it with equanimity. 'Very understandable,' he said soothingly. 'Glasses?'

Celia detached the glass from the carafe of water on the washstand and gave it to him.

'Penny doesn't go in for secret drinking. Or even public drinking,' she informed him chattily. 'This could be a challenge. Oh, what about the tooth-mug?'

She went into the bathroom. Penny found Zoltan was very close. He was laughing down at her, his amusement silent and undisguisable. She opened her mouth to remonstrate when, to her total astonishment, she was caught up in a whirlwind kiss. This time it did not feel as if he was experimenting to see if he liked it. Or demonstrating any other philosophical point. It was almost fierce.

'Where's your tooth-glass, Pen?' Celia called.

Penny put out a stunned hand to ease her hurried breathing. She had no breath to answer.

'Did Mrs Davies move it?' Celia called.

Penny closed her eyes, shutting out the unwelcome vision of Zoltan Guard's amusement and the imminent prospect of her sister walking in on them and drawing the all too obvious conclusion.

How dare he? she thought. But that was silly. She had only to open her eyes and view the matter of fact way with which he had returned to the champagne bottle to know exactly how he dared. Because he did not give a damn about what anyone thought.

'Oh, it's all right. I've found it,' Celia called.

Penny took three sharp steps backwards, leaving as much space between them as the furniture permitted. Her sister emerged triumphantly, bearing aloft the rose-covered tooth-mug Penny had owned since she was a child. She was shaking her head.

'Only one, though. Someone will have to drink out of the bottle.'

'I don't want any,' Penny said hastily.

Celia looked impatient. 'This is my wedding-day, for heaven's sake. You're going to have to indulge a bit today. It wouldn't be sisterly not to.' She held out the mug to Zoltan. 'Penny is virtually teetotal,' she explained, grimacing. 'Not so much as a glass of wine at Christmas. It's very boring.'

One of those heavy eyebrows flicked up. Penny knew he was storing it away, just as he had stored away every other damned thing she had told him since she met him off the train last night.

But he did not say anything. Instead he cast an experienced eye over her dressing-table and swooped. Unceremoniously tipping a tumble of trinkets on to the cloth-covered top, he presented her with an open lotus dish that Charles had brought back from China.

'There you are,' he said. 'You'll lose some of the bubbles but it will look wonderfully decadent.'

Celia giggled again.

He poured the wine for the three of them and then silently toasted Celia. They all drank, Penny barely sipping at hers.

'Wonderful,' said Celia after a long swallow. 'Oh, this is better than sitting and listening to Mummy complaining about how conventional Handel is.' She gave Penny a quick, conspiratorial look. 'Or anything else either.'

Zoltan's eyes narrowed.

Celia finished her drink and put down the tooth-mug. She peered in the mirror. The coronet of flowers was now distinctly lopsided.

'Well, if Mummy sees me now she really will have something to complain about,' Celia said cheerfully. She gave Penny a quick hug. 'Thanks for everything, Pen. You keep us all sane, you know. Oh, God, is that the time? I must *fly*.'

She whipped out of the door and let it crash behind her with a thump that sent dispossessed costume jewellery all over the floor. Penny groaned.

'She is very fond of you, isn't she?' Zoltan said in a thoughtful tone.

Penny was scooping up daisy earrings and a malachite ring.

'We're sisters.'

'Doesn't follow. I know sisters who are at each other's throats,' he said tranquilly.

'Well, we aren't. We've always got on very well.'

He was mildly surprised. 'Always? Even in your competitive teens?'

Penny laughed. 'I never competed with any of my sisters. We are too different. Leslie is brainy, Angel is dedicated to her dancing and Celia—well, you've seen her. She was always going to be the beauty of the family. Not much point in competing with her.'

She looked up, smiling. She was crouching on the carpet with the little trinkets in her hand. Just for a moment she surprised the oddest expression on his face. Almost as if he was angry. Her smile died.

But the expression was only there for a second. He sat down in her pretty painted cane chair. He should have looked ridiculous with his long booted legs propped against the feminine frills of the dressing-table. But he did not. In fact, Penny thought, startled, he looked as if he belonged there.

He smiled crookedly down at her.

'So when Celia was planning to be the beauty, what did you want to be when you grew up? A hospital administrator?' he asked with gentle irony.

Penny stood up, brushing carpet fluff off her robe.

'Of course not.'

'Well, then?'

There was something about the way he said it that convinced her he was not going to give up until he got his answer.

'I wanted to paint,' she said reluctantly.

'A painter,' he said thoughtfully. 'Did you go to college? Did you study it?'

She put the trinkets down carefully on the dressing-table.

'For a while.'

'What does that mean?'

She flung away from him. 'I didn't finish my course.'

It was odd, she thought, with the part of her mind that was not wincing away from the admission, how much that failure still hurt all these years later. She looked out of the window blindly, biting her lip. Below, the tradesmen's vans were beginning to leave, she saw.

'We ought to be getting ready.'

Zoltan ignored that.

'Was it your choice?'

Penny was watching the caterer's van as if her life depended on it.

'What?'

'That you didn't finish your art course,' he elucidated gently. 'Who took the decision? You or the college?'

What would he say if she told him the truth? Penny thought wryly. That neither she nor the college had decided. That Alan had come to the end-of-term exhibition, seen her work and the sales she had achieved, and had gone off on a bender of imperial proportions. That she had spent her twentieth birthday sitting by his bedside persuading him that he did not want to kill himself. That she had never gone back to college after that one, too-successful end-of-year show.

She shrugged, not answering.

But he was not to be deflected.

'Did you lose interest? Get bored?'

'There were other things I—wanted to do,' she said carefully.

Wanted! Well, she supposed she had wanted to then. She had been full of love and trust and optimism then. She had thought her love could cure Alan of his demon of alcoholism and his even deeper demon of jealousy.

Well, she had been wrong. She was no judge of men and no judge of her own emotional strength either. It was important to remember that, Penny thought.

'What other things?' said the soft, implacable voice behind her.

She shrugged again, not answering.

'How old were you?'

There seemed to be no harm in telling him. 'Twenty.'

'One year into that gambler's marriage of yours? Or less?'

Penny froze. She turned to face him. He was still sitting there, his boots on her dressing-table, looking at her over the top of his glass. He wore an expression of blandly social interest but she was not deceived.

'Why do you keep asking me things like that?' she said in sudden despair. 'Why do you keep digging and digging and digging? Why can't you leave me alone?'

'Why does it upset you so much?' he countered softly. 'All you need to do is tell me to mind my own business.'

'I have,' Penny said. She flopped down on the stool with a sigh. 'It didn't seem to work, as I recall.' She passed a hand over her hair in a distracted way.

'Do you still paint?'

'When I have time.'

'Ah.' He nodded thoughtfully. 'Another area of frustration. Your best energies going on stuff you don't believe in and only the time when you're tired left to paint. I can relate to that.'

Penny straightened. 'What do you mean, *another*...?'

He gave her an enigmatic smile.

She said hurriedly. 'Oh, good heavens, look at the time. We ought to be changing.' She remembered that sports bag and looked at him with misgiving. 'Will you—er—be changing?'

He laughed. 'There's plenty of time and you know it. Yes, I will be changing. I'm waiting for the iron.'

It was so unexpected that Penny was blank.

'What?'

'Iron,' he repeated calmly. 'The material is supposed to be crease-resistant but I'm sure your mother could tell. So I asked another of your sisters—Leslie, is it?—if I could borrow an iron to smarten it up a bit. I'm in a queue, I gather. We're stacked up until your father has dressed.'

Penny was surprised into a laugh.

'I bet you are.'

'Yes. I gather your mother was worried by his lack of progress,' Zoltan said.

His expression was neutral yet she knew he was laughing. Now, how do I know? Penny asked herself, bemused.

He stood up. Picking up the lotus dish she had put down on the dressing-table, he strolled across to her.

'You forgot your champagne.'

Penny took it. There didn't seem to be an alternative.

'I don't drink very much.'

'Less than a glass of champagne won't hurt you,' he said comfortably. 'It might even stop you looking as if you're expecting to be ambushed.'

'*What*?'

'It's not very flattering, you know.'

Penny was bewildered. 'I haven't the slightest idea what you're talking about.'

He smiled at her. 'Then let me show you,' he said
gently.

He put his hands out and grasped her by the shoulders.
Penny tensed. She began to pull away. But he was not
going to kiss her, she found. Instead he marched her to
the full-length mirror and stood her in front of it.

His hands looked very strong and tanned against the
old white robe. It was beginning to gape a little, Penny
saw, as the ancient belt relaxed its knot. She stood very
still in his hands, hoping it would get no worse.

He shook her very gently. 'Look at yourself, Penny
Dane,' he said softly. 'You should be in battledress with
a Kalashnikov in your hands. I've never seen a woman
so jumpy.'

Penny swallowed. She looked at the image in the
mirror; without make-up she looked ivory-pale, the green
eyes enormous. And, yes, he was right; her eyes were
full of wariness and a flinching knowledge of the possibility of hurt.

Lying, she said again, 'I don't know what you're
talking about.'

'Oh, I think you do. And I want to know why.'

In the mirror he seemed immensely tall and muscular
compared with her slenderness. She could feel the
warmth of him, the steady beat of his heart behind her
shoulderblade. She had not been this close to a man in
this room since she had left Alan. It would be so easy
to shift her weight a little, to lean back against him,
letting her head drop against his shoulder, the blonde
hair fanning out against the darkness of his shirt.

Her whole body seemed to sigh at the thought. So
easy. Dangerously easy.

Suddenly Penny could not bear it. She pulled out of
the light hold which was not—not quite—an embrace.

'We've got no time to play silly games. Let me go,'
she said in a stifled voice, although physically she had
already removed herself to the window.

He flung up his hands, palm outwards, laughing.

'You're free. I still want to know the answer.'

'You're imagining things. If I'm a little tense it's because there are a lot of things that can go wrong at weddings,' she said defensively.

'Yes, I considered that,' he agreed. 'But you like your future brother-in-law. There are no rivalries between you and your sisters. Your mother might be a bit overwrought but you're all used to it and you can handle it. So I ask myself, What is it that gives her that look of—desperation?'

Penny was startled. 'You're imagining it.'

Zoltan smiled. 'No.'

'But——'

'You've looked on the edge of desperation ever since I arrived last night,' Zoltan told her levelly. 'At first I thought it was because of me—you didn't know me, after all. A lot of women might find that a bit daunting, having to meet someone they didn't know and keep him entertained for a whole evening. But not you. That wasn't what worried you. You could handle it and a great deal more with one hand tied behind your back. Just as you handle me.' He was rueful.

'I don't,' protested Penny.

'Oh, but you do. You're very civilised about it, of course. Very hospitable, very polite. But every time we approach something you don't want to talk about, the notices go up. Protected area! It makes it very difficult to know what's going on in your head.'

Penny found she still had the lotus dish of champagne in her hand. In spite of her prejudices, she drank. It was cool and pleasant and the bubbles seemed to have a calming effect, she found gratefully.

'Why should you want to know what's going on in my head?' she said.

'It seems a reasonable first step.'

Her eyes widened. 'First step to what?'

'To wherever we're going.'

Penny did not pretend to misunderstand him. She did not think there would be much point. Zoltan Guard did not seem to care too much about the social niceties. He would certainly not let her get away with it.

She shook her head with decision. 'We're not going anywhere,' she said firmly.

'Oh, but we are,' he said with equal firmness. He seemed amused again.

Penny took another revivifying mouthful of champagne.

'You're mad,' she told him. 'We've known each other less than twenty-four hours. You asked me to go to bed with you and I said no. End of story.'

He chuckled. 'On the contrary. Start of story.'

'You mean that because I turned you down you have to keep after me till I agree?' Penny was incredulous. 'Oh, get real, please.'

'I told you, when I start a project I see it through to the end,' he told her tranquilly.

Penny glared. 'I am *not* a project.'

'Yes, you are. And likely to prove one of the most difficult I've ever set my hand to.' He sounded thoughtful.

'You will not set your hand to me,' she began hotly.

But there was another knock on the door. She jumped and fell silent, bewildered and indignant.

Zoltan took in her confusion, smiled at her with odious reassurance, and strolled over to the door.

It was Leslie. She was carrying coat-hangers.

'Pen, have you seen Mike's professor? I've ironed——'

She stopped short, taking in Zoltan's easy smile and her sister backed up against the window with flushed face and eyes darting green fire. If Penny looked hot and bothered, Zoltan looked completely at home. Leslie was flustered.

'Oh, I'm sorry,' she said. 'I didn't mean to interrupt.'

Penny did not say anything. Anything she could think of would only make it worse. Now there were two of her sisters who thought she was having a dance round the maypole with Zoltan Guard, she thought grimly. He, she could see, was well aware of the undercurrents—and hugely amused by them.

'How very kind,' said Zoltan smoothly. He took the coat-hangers from Leslie. 'I came to ask your sister if she would like me to drive to the church, since we will be going in the same car. I'm told that driving is ruin to smart high heels.'

'Er—how thoughtful,' said Leslie. She looked at Penny with faint anxiety. 'Are you all right, Pen?'

'I'm fine,' Penny said through clenched teeth. 'As you say, Professor Guard is all consideration.'

'Yes,' agreed Leslie, happily unaware of sarcasm. 'Steven wouldn't think of a thing like that.' She gave Zoltan an approving smile. 'Will you be long? Mummy's getting in a tizz and Daddy wants to give everyone a drink before we go off to church.'

'I've already had a drink,' said Penny. 'I don't want any more.'

Leslie's eyes widened slightly as she took in the champagne bottle. Her eyebrows rose but she contained her surprise. She prepared to go.

'Well, get a move on, anyway. Mummy wants to pin corsages on everyone. The bridesmaids have thrown her out and I think she's feeling a bit spare.'

'I'll be down as soon as I'm dressed,' Penny promised.

Leslie's eyebrows went a fraction higher. Zoltan met her startled gaze blandly.

'I also,' he assured Leslie, closing the door on her courteously but firmly.

His shoulders, Penny saw, were shaking with suppressed laughter.

'What's funny?' she said with uncharacteristic belligerence. 'Are you laughing at my family?'

He strolled over and took the lotus dish away from her.

'You really aren't used to alcohol, are you?' he said musingly. 'You can't have had more than a thimbleful and you're ready to do battle with the world already. I can see you're going to be a cheap date,' he added in self-congratulatory tones.

Penny choked. 'I am not going to be any sort of date...'

He just smiled.

'I'm not.' She was almost shouting. She had thought of a number of crushing things to say to the hateful man. So it was sad that the one that came out was the weakest. 'What would my family say?'

He threw back his head and laughed aloud at that.

'Why are you laughing? Don't laugh at me. I won't have you laughing at me,' she cried, taking a hasty step forward.

Her foot somehow got entangled with the hem of her robe. She stumbled. Zoltan caught her in a competent, unimpassioned embrace. He gently pushed the hair that had flopped forward out of her eyes.

'You don't have to fight me too, you know,' he told her, laughing quietly. 'If you're taking on the world, I'm on your side.'

'I am not——'

He held on to her. Quite suddenly she stopped resisting.

'What were you laughing at?' she muttered.

'At the idea that you cared what your family thought about you and me,' he told her, the sculpted lips twitching at the memory.

Penny was puzzled. 'Why?'

'Well, my darling, you've done your best to give them the impression that we have already reached an—er—accommodation.'

She stared up at him. He laughed softly.

'Did you think that your reputation for immunity would stand up to anything? Come on, Penny, be realistic. What would you think if you went into one of your sister's rooms and there she was swigging champagne with a man and wearing nothing but a robe that was on the point of falling off? What would your conclusion be in those circumstances, hmm?'

Penny took herself smartly out of his arms.

'How do you know I haven't got anything on underneath?' she demanded, her cheeks burning.

'Experience,' he said with deplorable sang-froid.

She tugged the robe so hard she almost wrapped it round her twice. All of a sudden she felt rather cold.

'I'm surprised you're not ashamed to admit it,' she said grimly.

'Are you?' He was interested.

She gave an exasperated sign. 'No. Not really. You're not ashamed of anything, are you?'

'If I'm not ashamed to do it, I'm not ashamed to admit it,' Zoltan said tranquilly. 'It's a very simple principle but it works. You should try it some time.'

'I don't do things I'm ashamed to admit,' Penny flashed.

'That wasn't quite what I meant,' he said drily. 'I mean, that policy doesn't leave a lot of room for you to do much, does it? You seem to be ashamed to admit such peculiar things.'

'I'm not. I'm an independent person and I do what I want——'

He was very close, she realised, breaking off.

Under her breath, not quite knowing why, she said, 'No.'

But it was too late.

CHAPTER SEVEN

ZOLTAN'S breath stirred the curling tendrils that lay against her throat. His body was not only muscular, it was alarmingly exciting—and it was between her and the door.

'Now, look,' said Penny, arching her throat to avoid his kiss, 'be sensible . . .'

'Sensible is no fun,' he murmured, turning his face into the fall of hair at the back of her neck. 'Your hair smells like the garden did last night. Mmm. I love English gardens.'

Penny gave a sweet, involuntary shiver. She repressed it.

'Thank you. That's because I've washed it,' she said, determinedly prosaic.

He gave a low laugh. She felt the small turbulence along the surface of her skin. In spite of herself she shivered again.

'You're amazing,' he said.

Every woman thought he was a knock-out, Mike had said. He knew what he was talking about, Penny thought in rising concern.

'I may be amazing. I am also unavailable,' she said firmly.

'Unavailable?' he murmured against the soft vulnerable skin below her ear. 'I don't think so, you know.' He kissed her throat lingeringly. 'I—really—don't—think—so.'

Her head fell back. In spite of herself, it seemed, her body was responding to him. And he knew it. Her pulse quickened.

Heaven help me, thought Penny.

130

She strove for a normal tone. 'Look, we really don't have time for this...'

Zoltan laughed huskily. 'How much time do you want, honey?'

Briefly Penny shut her eyes. 'My sister is getting married in less than an hour,' she said on a rising note. 'I'd like to be there.'

He raised his head. His eyes were as blue as the cobalt tube in her paintbox. They weren't laughing any more, Penny saw. She began to feel seriously alarmed.

As soon as he saw her expression, he smiled.

'Let me go,' she said breathlessly.

His smile widened. 'Persuade me.'

Penny felt horribly foolish. She turned her head away.

'I shouldn't need to,' she said in low voice.

He ignored that. 'Kiss me, Penny. Let's see where it takes us.'

Her breath fluttered in her throat at the thought. She winced.

'You're not exactly chivalrous, are you?' she said bitterly.

'No,' he agreed without noticeable regret. He pushed the robe away so that he could kiss her shoulder. 'I suspect too many men have been treating you with chivalry for too long. It gives you too big an advantage,' he murmured.

The feel of his lips on her skin made her shiver deep inside. Suddenly she felt silken, scented, precious...

'Oh, God,' said Penny under her breath. Even when she had been at her youngest and silliest and utterly dazzled by Alan, he had never made her feel like this.

'Kiss me,' Zoltan said again.

He raised his head. Their eyes met. She searched his face. There was no softness there. Just curiosity and a strange implacability which somehow she had almost expected.

'Why?' Penny said, almost to herself.

He shrugged. 'There is reason and there is need. This is not reason.' His eyes were intent. She had the feeling that he was looking into her deepest heart.

Penny could not look away. Time seemed suspended.

'Oh, lord,' she said at last on a long sigh.

At once his arms tightened. But there was no need. She was reaching for him eagerly. They kissed almost desperately.

He slid his arms under the robe. His fingers touched her spine, ran softly up and down it. Penny shivered in animal delight. She pressed closer, her hands nearly frantic in the crisp hair.

He was plucking the robe away. Helplessly, she dropped her arms from his neck. The unglamorous towelling slid silently to the floor. Penny swayed.

At once he gathered up. Before she knew what was happening he carried her to the bed and was beside her. He held her face between his hands and kissed her from chin to hairline and back, lingering at the corner of her mouth tantalisingly. Penny squirmed round, seeking his mouth. But he held her off, touching butterfly kisses all around her lips until she moaned deeply.

Then, as if she had pulled a trigger, Zoltan turned on his back and pulled her on top of him. His hand swept down her naked body in explicit demand. His hand was not entirely steady.

He's laying claim to me, Penny thought, shocked. She caught her breath. But she was too deep in the sensual delight to remember the principles that had got her through the last arid years. Too deep to remember basic common sense.

'Kiss me,' Zoltan said again. She thought that he too had forgotten everything except the fierce demands of the body.

And then, impossibly, unbelievably, there came another knock on the door.

Penny shot up on the bed as if someone had flung cold water over her.

'Pen? Pen? Are you in there?'

It was her mother. She looked round frantically for her robe. Any of her sisters would go away if she didn't answer, but Laura thought she was still licensed to walk into any of her daughters' rooms without permission.

'Just a minute,' she called. Her voice was so thick she hardly recognised it.

The robe was on the floor. She hauled it up. One of the sleeves had got itself inside-out. She was tousled and fiery-cheeked by the time she had her arms through both sleeves.

Zoltan was unmoved, she noted. He leaned back on one elbow, watching her with undisguised appreciation. In the circumstances, it was hardly tactful. It did nothing at all for Penny's self-possession as she wrenched the door open.

Fortunately the bed was masked from the door. She ran her hands through her disarranged hair.

'Darling!' Laura looked at her in dismay.

Penny looked down at herself in sudden horror. But the robe was in place and any tell-tale marks from those hectic moments in his arms were decently hidden under it. Her mother's expression was reaction to her state of unreadiness, she realised.

'I know. I know. I—forgot the time.'

On the bed, safely hidden from Laura, Zoltan grinned. Penny avoided his eyes at once. But she felt the colour rise in her cheeks.

'But, darling, we'll start leaving for the church any *moment*,' Laura said with pardonable exaggeration.

'Yes. I know. I'm sorry. I'll be downstairs in ten minutes,' Penny said desperately.

Laura looked dissatisfied. 'You'd better hurry. Shall I help you to dress?'

'*No!*' It was almost a scream.

Laura's eyes looked as if they were about to brim over. Clearly she had had the same treatment from Celia and the bridesmaids, Penny thought. Normally she would have relented and let her mother in. But in the circumstances it was out of the question.

Laura said, 'Darling you've done the flowers beautifully. But it's made you dreadfully late. You'll need someone to do your hair. It's a mess.'

She made as if to come in. Penny took a firm grip on the door. Zoltan flung himself back on the pillows and raised his hands in a gesture of surrender straight out of a hundred westerns.

He could afford to think it was funny, Penny thought sourly. He was not having to bar the door.

'No, Mother.'

'But——'

'Mother,' said Penny with the resolution of cold panic, 'you are holding me up. If you want me downstairs in ten minutes, go *away*.'

Laura blinked. Penny did not blame her. She had never spoken like that to her sweetly old-fashioned mother in her life. She closed the door firmly.

She turned back to Zoltan. His shirt was unbuttoned and hanging out of his jeans, she registered. She folded her lips together. She was not going to succumb to embarrassment now. For one thing there was no time. For another, she didn't see why she should feel embarrassment when Zoltan clearly regarded the whole thing as a huge joke.

She picked up the hangers with his suit on them from the chair where he had tossed them.

'There,' she said in an angry undertone. 'Take them and get out.'

In spite of the interruptions Penny was ready with time to spare. It was just as well. She found her mother tearful and her father impatient.

She also found that Zoltan was before her. He had changed into the pale suit. With it he wore a crisp midnight shirt that made his eyes look bluer than ever. The bridesmaids were impressed. Penny was less so. Especially when those eyes swept over her.

'Mmm. Very glamorous,' he murmured.

'Thank you,' she said coolly.

The silk dress was new, a swirl of arctic greens and apricot that echoed the gold lights in her hair. It also, Penny was registering now, flattered her slimness and her long elegant legs in ways she had not realised. When she had seen it at a design school exhibition she had fallen in love with it. She had thought that that was entirely because of the way it suited her colouring. Now, under Zoltan's amused appreciation, she became conscious of the way the soft stuff clung as she moved.

'Very demure,' he said. It sounded as if he was laughing privately. His eyes lingered at her breast, outlined too clearly for Penny's peace of mind by the exquisite cut of the dress. 'You're a very subtle lady, aren't you?'

The look in his eyes made her feel hot. There was more than laughter there. All of a sudden she remembered what it had felt like to be in his arms.

The trouble was it had felt so right. Not just warm and exciting but *right*. As if she was meant to be there. As if they shared all the tenderness in the world. As if she loved him.

Oh, no, thought Penny. Oh, no, I can't handle that. I can't have fallen in love with him. I can't. Not in this space of time. Not when I've put all that behind me. Not when all he wants is a brief fling. And only that at the instigation of my loving family.

Heaven help me get through this wedding, she thought, conscious of her eyes filling.

Zoltan looked at her consideringly. 'Why is that every time I pay you a compliment you look as if I've strapped you on the rack?' he asked.

Penny shifted her shoulders. 'You're imagining it.'

'No, I'm not.' He touched her lashes, retrieving an unshed tear with one long finger. Penny stared at him, startled. Their eyes met. He looked serious, the lurking laughter briefly banished. As she watched the handsome mouth twisted. He seemed to hesitate.

For a moment she thought he was going to kiss her, there in the crowded room with all her family and friends around them. She went very still. Half of her wanted him to, desperately. Half of her was sad. Not without love, she thought forlornly.

They were interrupted.

'Pen, you're a *genius*.' It was Celia, clasping her trailing woodland flowers. 'I've never seen anything so beautiful. Nothing the florists could have done would have been half so gorgeous.'

'Yes, it's lovely. So unusual,' said Laura, more dubiously.

Celia was her ebullient self again.

'I'll do the same for you next time,' she told Penny naughtily, before dancing away.

Laura shook her head. 'Oh, dear. She never thinks. Don't worry, darling.' She laid a soft hand on Penny's arm. 'You're very happy as you are. It's perfectly all right to be a professional woman on her own these days.' Her tone was, if anything, even more dubious. 'Oh, no, Minky darling, don't...'

She darted off to stop a junior bridesmaid eating her posy.

Beside her, Penny was aware of Zoltan laughing silently.

'There you are. You're licensed to get rid of your escort,' he said in her ear. 'I wish that didn't make me feel redundant.'

'Oh, God. Mothers,' she moaned. 'The embarrassment!'

'Think yourself lucky. My mother walked out when I was three and didn't walk back until my annual salary hit six figures. In dollars.'

She looked up at him sharply. He sounded indifferent enough but a thing like that would hurt, she thought.

Add it to exile at fourteen and the banker's daughter who had not loved him enough and you had a man who meant it when he said he was not into permanence.

Penny said gently, 'You haven't had a lot of luck with families, have you? Not like me.'

He said, 'I thought you thought your family was a pain.'

Penny said, 'I think you've taught me different.'

His eyes gleamed. 'You mean I'm reinstated as escort?'

She drew away. 'Don't push your luck,' she said lightly. 'I must see about the cars.'

There was the usual confusion as both her mother and her father had issued instructions. Penny sorted it out, had a brief word with Leslie and Angel, and was soon marshalling people into transport for the church.

Laura went with Angel and her husband. That left only Penny herself, and the two formal limousines for the bridesmaids and Celia and her father. She gave a long sigh. No disasters so far, she thought, as she went to her car.

'End of Act One,' an amused voice said in her ear.

She raised her head, startled.

'You haven't forgotten me?' Zoltan said reproachfully. He was leaning negligently against the open passenger door. He had obviously been waiting for her. 'You weren't really thinking of dispensing with my escort?'

There was a warmth around her heart. Penny found herself smiling at him unreservedly. As if they were already lovers, she thought, with a superstitious quiver in the throat. He held out an imperative hand.

'Come on, Cinderella, hand over the keys. I'm your coachman for the day.'

She surrendered them without a struggle. 'Heaven.'

He ushered her into the car as ceremonially as if he were a professional chauffeur.

'Tired?' he asked, swinging in beside her.

'A bit. I didn't sleep well,' she said without thinking. She encountered a wry look.

'Tell me about it.'

She fought down a blush. 'And all that rushing around this morning was a bit nerve-racking. Of course, if I'd realised I was in the hands of a professional management consultant, I wouldn't have worried.'

'Interesting. I would have said you'd be more likely to run me out of town,' Zoltan said drily. 'I didn't get the impression that you were exactly appreciative of my efforts this morning.'

'No, I wasn't very gracious. I'm sorry,' Penny said simply. 'I don't know what got into me.'

'Don't you?' he murmured. 'We must talk about that later.'

He put the car in gear. He drove with easy competence, Penny saw, as if he had been driving her ancient car all his life. He followed her directions to the church without fuss and slotted the car into the minimal space that had been left for it in a single powerful manoeuvre.

Watching the strong brown hands on the wheel, Penny felt that little shiver of awareness again, like the touch of a moth's wing. It was gone almost before she realised. But just for an instant she had remembered those hands on her body, had wondered what it would be like if he touched her again. It left her dry-mouthed and unsettled.

What is happening to me? she thought. I don't feel like this about men. Any men. I don't wonder about them touching me. I don't want to be touched. I don't like being touched.

But she had let Zoltan Guard touch her, she remembered. She had forgotten that she had disliked it, that it had left her feeling unsafe and vulnerable. She had wanted it. And it wasn't she who had stopped it.

If her mother had not knocked at the door then who knew what she would have wanted—or where it would have ended?

She did not meet his eyes as he helped her out of the car. She had the impression that he was laughing again, though.

He did not touch her. It was as if he knew he did not need to. As if he had picked up her thoughts and knew that she already carried his touch like a brand.

They walked into the church side by side. Penny was very conscious of the warmth of his body across the decorous distance that separated them.

All through the service she stayed conscious of him, though he was across the aisle.

She sat and stood and sang the familiar hymns mechanically. The ceremony she had not admitted she had been dreading flowed past her. Even the old words of the marriage vows, which always made her wince, did not hurt today. And when they came out into the sunshine she was dry-eyed.

'A beautiful service,' everyone said. 'A radiant bride.'

'Such a handsome man,' sighed old Mrs Carpenter sentimentally.

Penny looked at Zoltan where he stood talking to one of Mike's old university friends. The silver hair was dramatic against that even tan. The proud carriage of the head made him look like an emperor.

'Yes,' she agreed, swallowing. She tried to wrestle her reaction into something conventionally excusable. 'Of course, it's an unusual combination—white hair with such a young face. And those amazing blue eyes. Really blue eyes are always startling, aren't they?'

Mrs Carpenter looked at her oddly. 'I was talking about the bridegroom, dear,' she said.

'Oh,' said Penny, nonplussed. She flushed a little. 'Oh, yes, of course.'

'They make a handsome couple, don't they?'

They did. Penny agreed with just a hint of constraint. Mrs Carpenter went to kiss Celia while the photographer was chivvying the bridesmaids into a neat composition. Zoltan came back to her.

'You look flustered.'

Her eyes slid away from him. 'The church was hot,' she said defiantly.

The heavy brows rose. 'I thought it was distinctly cold in there.'

He was right. Penny shrugged. She was not going to explain the real reason for the discomfiture he detected.

'What are you wearing under that dress?' he asked, amused. 'Long woollen underwear?' He turned slightly, masking her from the crowd, and added in a mischievous undertone, 'That wasn't what it looked like to me.'

Penny felt her cheeks warm. She looked anywhere but at him, praying that the betraying colour would subside.

'That's not very funny,' she said, with an iciness worthy of her mother. 'Or in very good taste.'

Zoltan was unabashed. 'That depends on your point of view.'

Penny dared a single look at him. It was like flame.

'From my point of view,' she elucidated, 'I would prefer it if you did not refer to that unfortunate incident.'

She sounded like a Victorian governess, she thought in despair. She was not surprised when he chuckled.

'I just bet you would,' Zoltan agreed.

'Then don't.' She was crisp.

'Can't do that.'

'Why on earth not?'

'From *my* point of view,' Zoltan said gently, 'it wasn't unfortunate. Or an incident either, if by that you mean something that happens only once. I'm going to do my best to see it happens again. Preferably as soon as possible. Only next time I intend to make sure we aren't interrupted.'

Penny gasped. He laughed again. He took her cold gloved hand and slipped it into the crook of his elbow.

'Smile,' he advised. 'We're under observation.'

He was right. The official photographer was not the only man wielding a camera. Celia's godfather, for one, was crouching among the gravestones, directing an expensive lens in their direction. Hurriedly Penny adjusted her expression.

'Let go my hand,' she said under her breath, her smile fixed on the middle distance.

His only answer was to tighten his fingers perceptibly over her own.

'Let *go*.'

'Certainly not. No sensible man ever surrenders an advantage.'

So they were locked together when her mother came up. Laura had recovered but the aunt who accompanied her was still distinctly damp around the eyes.

'Such a lovely service,' she said. 'So touching.'

'They always are,' Laura said, with a touch of sharpness.

Penny swallowed suddenly. She had not cried in church. But the memory of the soft look on Celia's face as she spoke the old vows caught her suddenly by the throat. Her mother looked at her narrowly.

'It's certainly powerful stuff,' Zoltan agreed easily. 'In any language.'

The elderly aunt looked at him with approval.

'I understand you aren't married, Professor?' she said, avoiding Penny's indignant eye.

Zoltan grinned. 'Never have been. Too big a risk.'

That would not shock Aunt Mary as much as he probably expected, Penny thought with a certain satisfaction. She had married off three adventurous and reluctant sons herself.

Sure enough, Aunt Mary was saying serenely, 'That just means you haven't met the right woman yet.'

Penny had underestimated him, she found. The handsome face stayed calm, politely interested. True, a faint tremor ran through the arm under her fingers. But whether it was a superstitious shudder or pure amusement she could not tell. She suspected the latter.

She was certain of it when he said gravely, 'You could be right.'

Penny ground her teeth and hauled as unobtrusively as she could manage at her hand. To no avail. Aunt Mary's eyes sharpened.

Laura said, 'Darling, we must go and line up for the family picture.'

Zoltan let her go then. But not before he had raised her hand to his lips and sent a sizzling look down the length of her arm. It made Penny long to hit him. It also sent Aunt Mary's eyebrows up to the brim of her hat and brought a worried frown to Laura's brow.

'Darling,' she said again.

The photographs took a long time. The May winds tossed hats and veiling about unpredictably. The photographer's professional amiability grew strained. By the end Penny was shivering in her silk dress.

She retreated to the shelter of a holly bush while the final shots were taken.

'Let's go,' said a familiar voice in her ear.

She jumped. He took her arm masterfully.

'Come on.'

'I can't,' she said. She looked wistfully at the church door where her father had one arm wrapped round Celia and the other placed on the shoulder of his new son-in-law while her mother and sisters looked on. 'My family... I ought to wait for them.'

'You're cold,' he said crisply. 'Wait for them at the house.'

'But——'

'They want any more snapshots of you, they can take them in front of the radiator,' he said. 'I'm taking you back.'

It was too tempting. Penny went with him without a struggle.

In the car he said, 'Poor old Cinderella. You just don't have any self-defence at all, do you?'

'What do you mean?'

'There you are jumping again whenever your family clap their hands.' He sounded annoyed.

Penny sighed. 'You don't understand. It's a convention to wait for the bride and groom to leave the church first.'

He slanted a look down at her. 'Even when you're incubating pneumonia?'

'I'm not——' She broke off as she was overtaken by a deep shiver she could not attempt to disguise. 'Damn,' she said.

He laughed. Reluctantly Penny smiled.

'Do you never get tired of being right?' she asked.

The blue eyes gleamed. 'So you agree I'm always right?'

She remembered their earlier encounter. And his conviction that she was not unavailable, in spite of her claim. She felt the faint colour rise in her cheeks and was grateful that his eyes were on the road.

'You clearly think so,' she said repressively. 'Personally I doubt it.'

'That's because you haven't known me long enough,' he said soothingly.

Penny allowed herself a mocking laugh. 'That's a matter of opinion,' she muttered.

He shook his head. 'You'll see.'

She eyed him unflatteringly. 'There's nothing wrong with your ego, is there?'

'There's nothing wrong with any of me,' he said superbly. 'It was your lucky day when you found me, Cinderella.'

'Somehow I doubt that,' Penny said, thinking of the maternal reproaches she would face for leaving the church early.

'You'll see,' he said again.

Penny didn't answer. She was learning that you did not get the better of Zoltan Guard by argument. The only possibility was avoiding action.

Accordingly she retired to her room as soon as they got back to the house. She sat in front of the mirror and retouched her make-up carefully. No need to add blusher, she saw ruefully. She did not emerge until there was enough noise to proclaim that the party was in full swing.

When she came downstairs her parents and Mike and Celia were still in the receiving line, greeting the last arrivals. But everyone else was circulating in the flower-decked rooms. The scullery already showed several cases of empty champagne bottles and the hired waiters were spinning in and out of the kitchen as if battery-powered.

Penny helped herself to a champagne flute and a bottle of fizzing mineral water. She entered the drawing-room unobtrusively and lodged the bottle of mineral water behind an urn of trailing roses. Other family weddings had taught her that if you wanted to drink and didn't want to drink alcohol then it was a good idea to set up your own private cache.

She looked round for her sisters. They were deeply engaged with old friends or new acquaintances. She did not admit that she was looking for Zoltan Guard as well but she located him anyway. He was talking to a couple of men she did not recognise. Friends of Mike's, obviously. Maybe fellow former pupils of Zoltan's. Penny turned away, telling herself she was relieved that her escort duties seemed to have come to an end.

Now it was time for other duties. She straightened her shoulders and began to circulate conscientiously.

It was a big wedding. The party seemed to go on for ever, Penny thought. She talked and drank her mineral water and stood on elegant heels until her head rang with the noise, her throat tasted like a vitamin pill and her feet ached. If only she could leave now. But there was the meal and the speeches to come. Briefly alone, she thought longingly of Zoltan's cavalier way with wedding conventions.

'Let me take you away from all this,' said a voice in her ear. She was coming to know that note of amusement all too well.

Penny choked. For some reason her heart gave a convulsive jump at the unexpected words. She had not even known he was anywhere in the vicinity. Or had she? It was uncanny the way she had been thinking about him just the moment before he spoke, she thought.

Penny coughed hard, cleared her throat, and mopped watering eyes. She brought her breathing back under control. She took a fortifying swig of mineral water and turned to face him.

'I seem to have heard that before,' she said.

'You'll be hearing it again,' Zoltan said, amused.

The blue shirt really was startling, the way it was reflected in his eyes. And brilliant blue eyes smiling straight down into your own were a disconcerting experience, Penny found.

'You have a one-track mind?' she asked faintly.

He considered the point.

'I've never thought so. You seem to have a peculiar effect on me,' he told her with candour.

Penny recovered herself. She raised her brows. 'Should I be flattered?'

'That rather depends on whether you like having that effect on me.'

She snorted. '*Like* it? You think I mean to encourage you to make fun of me?'

'I'm not making fun of you, Cinderella.'

She sighed. 'What else would you call it?'

Just for a moment he seemed to hesitate. She tipped her head on one side to look at him, her whole attitude a challenge. He looked back at her, his mouth slanted in a wry expression.

'I think we need more time for this discussion. And some privacy,' he said, a rueful note in his voice.

For a moment Penny did not understand him. When she did, she took an involuntary step backwards, her amusement dissolving in a quick response to a danger signal. The blue eyes narrowed, taking in that instinctive retreat.

'Complete privacy.' His voice was suddenly steely.

Penny was saved from having to answer by the announcement of the meal, set out in the marquee in the garden. She was seated at the same table as Zoltan but at a distance. She did not know whether that was a relief or an annoyance. She only knew that her first feeling was of sharp disappointment.

Careful! she said to herself. He'll be gone by tonight or tomorrow at the latest. And, no matter what he says about attraction, the first thing he told you was that it was purely temporary. Remember that!

She concentrated hard on her neighbour, a distant cousin of her new brother-in-law's.

Once or twice she looked up and found Zoltan looking at her. There was a faint frown between the black brows. She shivered a little, although it was anything but cold in the big tent. She did not think anyone had ever looked at her with such serious intentness before. It was as if he wanted to have all her secrets laid bare for him.

She looked away. Well, he was not going to. Nobody knew all her secrets. She had worked hard to banish them to outer darkness. No casual philanderer was going to bring them roaring back into the light.

There were speeches. Penny listened with half an ear to her father's polished performance. It set in stark contrast Mike's brief, embarrassed speech, to say nothing of the best man's rambling tissue of drunken innuendo. She winced inwardly. Even these days it brought back other drunken ramblings, without the hearty laughter and friendly goodwill. It was an effort to smile, though she applauded conventionally when the best man was at last persuaded to sit down by his amused well-wishers.

Throughout it all, she was conscious of Zoltan. Not that he was looking at her all the time. In fact, thought Penny ruefully, she seemed to be more conscious of him when he was paying attention to his neighbour, a vivacious redhead who borrowed a studio in the summer.

Get a hold on yourself, she told herself. It doesn't matter to you who he talks to. After today you'll never see him again. And just as well.

Tables began to break up. The men on either side of her went to join their girlfriends. Penny pushed the uneaten food away from her and looked at her watch. She was conscious of a faint throbbing at her temples.

'There you are,' said a voice above her head. Not Zoltan's for once, Penny thought in quick amusement. This was slightly slurred, very friendly and not in the least dictatorial. She looked up with a smile.

It was the inebriated best man. He collapsed on to the little gilt chair beside her and helped himself absentmindedly to her untouched glass of champagne.

'Wonderful wedding,' he said, beaming.

Penny tensed. She could not help herself. It was an instinctive reaction that she supposed she would never now get rid of. But he was a nice enough man when sober and his present intoxication was not taking a threatening form. So she calmed her pulses and kept her smile in place.

'I'm glad you're enjoying it.'

'Got a bit worried about m'speech,' he confessed. 'Glad it's over.'

Penny could appreciate that. He looked at her expectantly. Clearly words of appreciation were called for.

'It was a very friendly speech,' she said diplomatically.

He was pleased. 'Mike and I—friends since school. Even went to university together.'

'Oh?' She sought for a neutral topic. One presented itself. 'Do you know his old tutor, then? Professor Guard?' she asked casually.

'Old Zoltan?' The beaming smile became a beacon. 'Course I know Zoltan. Used to recycle his girlfriends when he'd finished with them.'

'*What*?' Penny did not believe she could have heard aright.

But her cheerful companion nodded. 'Devil of a fellow, old Zoltan. All the girls used to fall for him. Never had a girl student who didn't.'

Penny found she was not surprised. Zoltan's whole manner had indicated as much. It must have taken years of sexual negotiation to perfect that elegant technique. So why did she feel somehow betrayed by this information? It was no more than she would have expected if she had thought about it.

She said in a chilly voice, 'And you took the surplus off his hands?'

The best man detected something wrong. He blinked at her.

'Made an awful nuisance of themselves, some of them,' he offered as a palliative. 'Used to lie in wait for him when he came home. Smuggle themselves into his room. The works.' He contemplated their shared past with evident regret. 'Never seen anything like it. One girl wrapped herself round him like a boa constrictor. Took two of us to get her off.'

Penny stiffened. She had responded to Zoltan in a way she could not remember responding to anyone in her whole life, ever. Would this uncomplicated young man have described her as a boa constrictor? She had an uneasy feeling that he would. She gritted her teeth. It was unnerving to find that she was one of an army.

'He must have been grateful for your help,' she said acidly.

He looked doubtful. 'Soft-hearted chap. I said to him once, "Zoltan," I said, "you can't let these silly little creatures take over your life." But he could never bring himself to say a rude word to them, even when they were mega-inconvenient. Used to feel sorry for them, I suppose.'

Penny winced. Not that Zoltan Guard had any reason to be sorry for her, she reminded herself. He might call her Cinderella; he might even detect that she carried secret scars but at least for the moment he had no idea what they were. And it was going to stay exactly like that, she promised herself.

The best man had finished her champagne. He reached out for the bottle in the middle of the table and emptied it into the glass he had appropriated. At the same time he shifted the fragile chair closer to hers.

'Always make me feel sentimental, weddings,' he confided.

His smartly trousered leg pressed uncomfortably against hers. Penny changed her position unobtrusively.

'Do you go to a lot of them?'

'Weddings? All the time. M'friends are falling like flies these days,' he told her.

He downed his wine. He was watching her somewhat muzzily over the top of the glass.

'You married?'

Penny hesitated.

'I'm not,' he said encouragingly.

He had clearly misinterpreted the reason for her hesitation. She needed to deflect his attention from herself. Choosing her words carefully, Penny said lightly, 'Never found the right woman?'

He looked briefly morose. 'Oh, I've found her. She——' he hiccuped suddenly '—she wants another chap.' He shook his head, banishing depression. He replenished his drink and returned to the subject that interested him. 'What about you? Found the love of your life?'

'Found and lost and it's all a long time ago,' Penny said firmly.

'Loved and lost,' he said, enlightened.

The pressure of his thigh against hers was abruptly renewed. He was almost pushing her off her chair. Penny leaned away from the fumes of champagne.

'You—broken heart. Me—broken heart,' he pronounced.

He put his face close to hers. There was a faint sheen of sweat on his forehead. This had the makings of a full-blown scene, she thought, her heart sinking.

'My heart is not broken,' she said in a voice like ice-water.

But he wasn't listening any more. He was touching. Penny pushed his hand away. He hardly seemed to notice. He was trying to focus on her eyes, she saw. The insistent hand returned to fumble at her smart silk.

Penny felt cold. She looked round. But everyone was occupied—talking and laughing, toasting each other. Nobody was looking at them. Nobody was going to come over and distract him. She was going to have to deal with the man unaided.

Oh, well, she had had plenty of practice, she thought grimly.

She pushed the slender chair back with a sudden jerk. It startled him. For a moment his hand fell away.

'You need some air,' she told him.

A strange expression crossed his face—half cunning, half sulky. He leaned forward and took hold of her chair, his arms on either side of her, pinning her in place. Penny could smell the wilting carnation in his buttonhole. His breath reeked of the wine. She turned her face away, her mouth twisting in reflex disgust.

Too much practice, she thought. She knew from bitter experience what was all too likely to happen next. And her fellow guests would not be able to ignore it, either.

'Please leave me alone,' she said.

She strove to appear calm, although her nails were digging into her palms and her neck ached with the strain of avoiding that greedy touch. It was important to stay calm, not to let her fear and disgust show. Not to give him cause to hurt her.

'Don't mean that,' he said.

It was just what Alan had always said.

In spite of her sensible resolutions, Penny laughed.

An ugly light flashed in his eyes. In a split-second she realised she had made a mistake. Suffused with drink and affront, the heavy face swooped on hers. She tried to break free. But her momentary hesitation had lost her the chance. Unsteady hands took hold of her in a convulsive grip and his breath filled her mouth. Penny felt the horror close down over her. She made a small, high sound of distress like a wild creature about to be mauled.

And then, unbelievably, she was free.

She had closed her eyes instinctively. Now she opened them. Her tormentor was being helped to his feet by Zoltan Guard. He was looking bewildered. Somehow, his chair had toppled over sideways. The helpful Professor Guard was restoring the furniture to an upright position as well. He was smiling.

'Hi, Ian. Great to see you. How's life?'

The best man shook his head. In order to face Zoltan he had to turn his back to Penny. Slowly she let out the breath she had hardly been aware she was holding. Her fists uncurled. Cautiously she stood up. She was shaking badly.

Zoltan flicked her a glance over the best man's shoulder. Penny revised her opinion abruptly. He was not smiling. His mouth was curved pleasantly enough but the blue eyes were blazing. He was furious.

CHAPTER EIGHT

THE best man was despatched smoothly. You could see
the professional who was used to dealing with difficult
students, Penny thought.

'What you need,' Zoltan was saying sympathetically,
'is a coffee. Black coffee. They're hiding the coffee urn
over there, behind the potted palm.'

The other looked at him blearily. 'You're a good sort,
Zoltan,' he said. He clearly had no idea he was being
got rid of.

'Coffee,' said Zoltan, turning him in the right direction
and giving a gentle push to his shoulders.

Penny watched him go. Her breathing slowly returned
to normal. She put a hand to her throat.

'Thank you,' she said in a subdued voice.

Zoltan turned back to her. She looked up at him candidly. With a little shock, Penny realised that the calm,
easy voice had been a complete deception. The blue eyes
were molten with anger.

'What the *hell*,' he said, fury ripping through the quiet
voice, 'do you think you were doing with that drunken
fool?'

Penny blinked. 'I'm sorry?'

'So you should be.' He was curt. 'How could you let
that happen? You're not a child.'

She stared, taken aback. She felt half insulted, half
uneasy. How had Zoltan managed to notice what was
going on when nobody else in the room had been aware
of it? And, more important, why had he noticed? Be
careful! her heart warned.

She tried a half-lie. 'What do you mean? Nothing
happened.'

His hand shot out and took her by the elbow.

152

'Then why are you trembling?'

Penny jumped. His touch was electric. She looked round, disconcerted. He made her feel very vulnerable.

'Stop it,' she hissed, reaching for the conventions to armour her. 'People are staring.'

'No one is taking a blind bit of notice,' Zoltan corrected calmly. He shook her elbow a little and repeated, 'Why are you trembling?'

There was no point in saying that she wasn't. The evidence was there for him to feel in the faint tremor of her flesh under his hard fingers. Penny sought for a reasonable explanation.

'You—startled me.'

He looked down at her for a moment. One eyebrow flicked up.

'You're saying it's my fault you're shaking like a leaf?'

She looked pointedly down at the hand on her arm.

'Oh, no,' he said softly. 'You're not getting away with that. I remember what you look like when I touch you.' The blue eyes bored into hers. 'Not sick,' he said deliberately. 'Not scared to death either.'

Penny flushed. Her eyes fell under his harsh inspection.

'You want to know what I think?' he went on in a conversational tone. 'I think Ian scared you out of your mind. I think if I hadn't stopped it when I did, you'd have passed out.'

Penny was shocked. Her eyes flew to his, horrified.

'I wouldn't,' she said in a suffocated voice.

'No? You had your eyes screwed tight shut and you looked like a ghost. In fact, I've seen more colour in a snowfield.' He paused. 'I think you were so scared you were frozen to the spot,' he said softly.

It was uncomfortably close to the truth. Penny's eyes skittered away from his.

'If that's what you think then you don't sound very sympathetic about it,' she managed at last, with rather shaky sarcasm.

'Sympathetic? Because you let yourself be terrorised by a drunken boy?' Zoltan sounded incredulous. 'Of course I'm not sympathetic. You should have got yourself out of it as soon as you realised what state he was in.'

It was so much what Penny herself had been feeling—and failing to achieve—that she burned with resentment.

'How could I?' she flashed. 'He's one of the honoured guests. I couldn't haul off and box his ears. It would spoil the party.'

Zoltan looked amused suddenly. 'I would have said it was more likely to make it, from what I recall of Mike and Ian and their cronies.'

'Then they differ from my sister Celia,' Penny retorted. 'To say nothing of my mother.'

He looked impatient. 'It's academic anyway. You wouldn't have had to lay him out cold. You're a sophisticated woman. You know how to deflect a man without resorting to violence. You did it to me easily enough,' he reminded her, an undercurrent of laughter stirring the smooth voice.

Penny bit her lip. 'That was different.'

'How?'

She glared at him. 'You weren't drunk,' she said, goaded.

'But I was much more serious——' He broke off suddenly. His eyes narrowed.

Her uneasiness increased by the second. Not for the first time, Penny was aware of an acute brain at work behind his neutral expression. He looked her up and down. Not as he had done before. This time it was almost absent, as if he was trying to see where a rather small Penny fitted into some large geometrical pattern that he had in his mind's eye.

'Drunk,' he said slowly.

Out of the crowd someone came up to him. They touched him on the shoulder, said something. He barely moved.

'Hi,' he said, not taking his eyes off her. 'Catch you later.'

The man moved off. Penny began to feel like a laboratory specimen under that implacable analysis.

'I wish you'd stop looking at me like that,' she muttered, protesting.

'Drunk,' he repeated, ignoring it.

'And let me have my arm back.'

He ignored that too. He was looking at her as if he were a chemist who had just found a new element.

'Even last night—when your father came in. You weren't scared when we were running through the garden after unknown intruders. But you were scared then, when he came in. I felt it. You went rigid.'

'No,' said Penny, appalled.

How could he tell? How *could* he?

'I didn't understand it. He's not the sort of tyrannical father a girl would be afraid of, your dad. And you're not the type to be afraid of a tyrant anyway. You're too cool. Too competent.'

'Of course I'm not afraid of him,' she said hotly. But her heart was cold with trepidation.

'No, I guess not. But you were afraid of *something*.'

'I——' She shrugged helplessly.

'He'd been drinking with his agent,' Zoltan said slowly. 'He'd had just a little too much. He was rather charming about it. And he wanted another drink. Only you hustled him off to bed.'

'He needed to be up at a reasonable hour today...'

'And you didn't want him to have any more alcohol.' He watched her. 'That's what you're afraid of, isn't it? Did you think he'd get really drunk? Go out of control?'

Penny thought, he's very nearly there. He's just a couple of steps away from knowing all there is to know about me. She had never felt so naked in her life.

She said numbly, 'No.'

'There's no need to be ashamed of it,' he said, with surprising gentleness. 'He wouldn't be the first overworked actor to have a drink problem. And if he has it's hardly your fault.'

'He hasn't.'

Zoltan looked at her narrowly. Penny bit her lip. But in the end he obviously decided that in this, at least, she was telling the truth.

'Then——'

Penny took a decision. If she didn't give him some sort of explanation, Zoltan Guard was going to keep worrying away at the problem until he got the right answer, she thought. He liked puzzles too much to let it go. The more difficult they were, the better he liked them. It didn't matter that people might get hurt while he solved them to his intellectual satisfaction.

But she was not a fool. She could tell him something that would satisfy him. Admit the symptom, she thought wryly, and with a bit of luck he won't dig too deep for the cause. And then it can stay my secret.

'Look,' she said, with a great air of frankness, 'I'm a bit worried by people who have had even just a little too much to drink. I'm not proud of it. But I can't help it. I do try to control it. It's a sort of phobia, I suppose.'

'Why?'

Penny jumped. 'What?'

'Phobias have origins,' Zoltan pointed out. 'Where did you pick up yours? And why?'

So much for him not digging for the cause! Penny thought up her answer with lightning speed.

'If you work in a big London hospital you learn to be afraid of drunks,' she told him.

It was even true, she thought, momentarily pleased with herself.

But his eyes stayed watchful.

'You learned to be afraid of drunks in your work?'

She looked away. 'They can be violent. You never know what they're going to do next.' In spite of herself her voice trembled.

Against her will she remembered Alan's face. Too vividly. It sprang to life as she had last seen it, his lips caught back from his teeth in a snarl that was more animal than human. He had not even recognised her by then, she thought. Involuntarily she shivered.

Zoltan said softly, 'I don't believe you.'

Penny jumped and blinked. 'There are studies...'

He dismissed the studies with a shrug. 'I am not quarrelling with you about the typical behaviour of alcoholics. Just about where you learned to fear it.'

At that she was silenced.

The noise of the wedding party swirled and rose all around them. People were enjoying themselves, Penny thought. The hum of conversation was punctuated by laughter. It was all very friendly, very normal.

It might have been a million miles away for all the good it did her.

Penny looked into assessing blue eyes and felt as if she had been abandoned on an ice planet with an alien life-force. A terrifyingly intelligent alien life-force.

He said gently, 'Before I came along just now, you looked as if you were in the middle of a nightmare. And poor old Ian is no werewolf.'

To her horror she felt her throat close with tears.

'I never thought he was,' she said in a choked voice.

It was the gentleness that did it, she thought, scrabbling for a handkerchief. If Zoltan had carried on glaring at her like the Grand Inquisitor then she wouldn't have dissolved in this embarrassing way. She sniffed and tried to pretend that her eyelashes were not wet.

He said something under his breath. She could not make out what it was. It could have been in a foreign language. Or it could just have been exceptionally rude. It sounded fierce.

'We need to get out of here,' he said abruptly.

Penny had found her handkerchief. She blew her nose hard.

'We can't. They'd notice. My mother would never forgive me.'

He gave her an ironic look.

'Oh, all right,' she said crossly, interpreting the look correctly. 'It doesn't matter what my mother thinks.'

'Not just at this precise moment, no,' he agreed.

Zoltan began to move forward purposefully. With a numb Penny held firmly by the wrist, he cleared a path for them through the press of people. Penny noticed the way people seemed just to move aside for him, as if he had only to look in a certain direction and all obstacles removed themselves.

Just like my defences, she thought, worried. What privacy am I going to have left when he has finished dissecting my innermost feelings?

But she still went with him. He was like a stormforce wind. You just bent with it or you broke, she reasoned.

He led her unerringly to the door of her own apartments. It was as if he had lived in the rambling house all his life instead of a matter of hours. But of course he already knew how to find her bedroom. No doubt he had laid out the map of all routes to her door as soon as he arrived, Penny thought bitterly.

He closed the outer door and locked it. Then he took her up to the sun-filled sitting-room.

Penny looked at him warily.

'Brilliant navigation.'

'I can find my way round most places. It's a skill you need if you're a permanent stranger.' He smiled. 'Sit down and relax. I'm not going to jump on you.'

She lifted her chin. 'I never thought you were.'

He considered her for a thoughtful moment. 'No you didn't, did you. You're—an unusual woman, Penny Dane.'

'Why? Because I don't think of you as the big bad wolf?'

She was rather proud of her tone. It not only successfully suppressed the threatening tears, it sounded like the last word in careless sophistication.

She went on, 'I would have thought it was obvious. You can hardly give me a lecture on decent behaviour and then jump on me yourself,' she added, genuine amusement dawning.

Now that they were away from the crowd and her lurching best man antagonist she was feeling better by the moment.

Zoltan's strongly marked eyebrow flicked up. 'Is that what I was doing? Lecturing you on your behaviour?' He sounded faintly annoyed.

'That's what it felt like,' she said firmly.

'I must be losing my touch,' he said in a dry tone.

She sat down on an eighteenth-century couch with a pretty curved back and looked up at him in mockery.

'Would you *rather* I looked on you as the big bad wolf?'

The blue eyes narrowed. Definitely annoyed now, Penny thought. She felt rather pleased with herself. A great deal of her confidence returned abruptly. He might not want her to think of him as an ogre but glamorous Professor Guard didn't want her dismissing him as a pussycat either.

He said with something of a snap, 'I'd rather you saw what was going on under your nose.'

She crossed one leg over the other, clasped her hands round her upraised knee and leaned back. She felt relaxed and almost in control again.

'You think I'm missing something?'

'If you think I give a damn about your good behaviour then you're certainly missing something.' He sounded almost grim.

Penny widened her eyes at him.

'Then why did you rush me out of the party like that?'

He stared at her for a long moment. Then he said slowly, 'Because I thought, God help me, that you needed rescuing. And not just from Ian Springer.'

Penny was silenced. Her mocking confidence faltered. Unwillingly she searched his face, and saw that he was telling the truth. All the mockery drained out of her. She felt cold and vulnerable again. It was not a feeling she welcomed.

She was *not* vulnerable, she reminded herself. She had learned to take care of herself. She had been taking care of herself quite successfully for more than five years now.

She looked away.

'Why should you care?' she demanded at last in an exasperated voice. 'Even if you were right and I did need rescuing—what has it got to do with you? I only met you last night. After the wedding we're most unlikely to meet again. Why did you have to interfere? Why couldn't you leave me alone?' To her consternation, her angry voice broke in the middle of the last word.

'Is that what everyone else does?'

'What?'

Zoltan was looking at her gravely. 'Leaves you alone. You're a pretty solitary lady, aren't you?'

Penny stared. 'What do you mean?'

'The one who doesn't like parties,' he reminded her softly. 'The one who stays behind to meet the unknown guest.'

'Don't start that Cinderella business again,' Penny said dangerously. 'I told you——'

'The one nobody notices any more.'

It stopped her dead. She stared at him in consternation.

He said into the silence, 'The one who takes good care that nobody notices her. I ask myself why.'

She said with an effort, 'You're imagining it.'

Zoltan was unruffled. 'I don't think so.'

Penny met his eyes and read determination in them. She clasped her arms round herself, suddenly cold.

'Let us examine the facts,' he said.

He sounded mildly interested, as if she were some academic subject on the fringe of his discipline, Penny thought in dawning indignation. She did not delude herself, though. However mild his interest, he was not going to leave it now until he got to the bottom of the riddle. She was looking at years of careful defences being breached in less than twenty-four hours, she thought. And all because he found weddings boring and was looking for distraction. This wasn't what Sue Flynn had meant by the wedding effect, but it was going to be just as deadly to her peace of mind.

He cast a comprehensive look round her room. 'You moved in here after you married?'

Penny moistened her suddenly dry lips.

'We couldn't really stay in my old room in the main house. It wasn't big enough.'

His quick look told her that he had noted the evasion.

'But you and your husband lived here? In your parents' house?'

That had been the start of the problem, Penny often thought. Alan had said he wanted to stay there. They didn't have to pay rent to her parents and it was the ideal spot for painting. But it hadn't worked out like that. It hadn't worked out like that at all.

'Some of the time,' she said uncommunicatively.

He let that one go. Instead he looked round the room eloquently.

'He didn't leave much of a mark, did he? What did you do? Clear everything out that reminded you of him? When did you do that? When he died? Or before?'

'How——?' She stopped. Too late. She had been going to ask how he could tell. His expression told her he knew that, in spite of her cutting it off before it was articulated.

His mouth tilted. It was all the answer he was going to give her, she realised. They stared at each other like duellists. The silence hummed with her antagonism.

'When he left,' Penny said at last, curtly.

'It was traumatic?'

She remembered all too clearly. The answer was written on her face.

His voice was unemotional. 'What happened?'

She stood up and moved restlessly to the window. She could feel his eyes on her. The afternoon sun was filling the courtyard with light, turning the old house to honey and the creeper round the door to a flourish of embroidery. It all looked unutterably peaceful. Penny looked at it blindly.

In her mind's eye all she could see was the ill-lit kitchen in the squalid south London flat. The move had been a last-ditch stand to save their marriage. She had been desperate to get away from the claustrophobic atmosphere, with her mother watching every time Alan went out and then telling her exactly how long he had spent away from his canvas. Alan had known the move was necessary as much as she did. But he had still hated it.

Penny closed her eyes, remembering. She could still see the threadbare carpet and the tangle of stained cloths, the smeary canvases that Alan had left in his wake that night. That last terrible night. The night she had promised herself she would never tell anyone about.

She said in a voice as unemotional as Zoltan's own, 'Alan was having trouble with his painting. We—had had difficulties for some time.'

Behind her, she heard him move. Her spine tensed. But he did not approach or speak. That helped. She clasped her hands in front of her and opened her eyes.

'He had been drinking. He drank a lot. Well, I think you've guessed that. He was drinking more and more. I was worried but I didn't realise——'

She broke off. She brushed a strand of blonde hair off her face. Her voice became a shade less steady. 'You don't readily say to yourself, My husband is an alcoholic. Alcoholics are other people. People you read about in newspapers. Not someone you live with every day.'

He said, 'There are usually signs.'

'Oh, there were those all right. Mood swings. Terrible rages. The depression. Sometimes complete withdrawal. There were times when he would go out and not come back for three or four days. I thought——' She bit her lip. 'I thought it was my fault.'

His voice was level. 'Those difficulties you were talking about?'

She flushed. 'Yes.'

'What was wrong between you?' It was still that neutral voice. If it hadn't been, she probably wouldn't have told him.

'He said I had everything. Scholarship to art school. Enough money to live. Friends. Family.' She paused and then added in a low voice, 'He didn't, you see. He ran away from home when he was a schoolboy. After that he was on his own.'

'And you felt you owed him because of it?'

'No!' It was an instinctive, immediate protest, almost a cry of pain. Genuinely shocked, Penny heard it hanging in the air between them.

'I think you did,' he said softly.

This was horrible. She shook her head almost frantically. 'You know nothing about it.'

His mouth tightened. 'I'm willing to bet I know a damn sight more about it than anyone else.' His voice was harsh.

Her head reared up. 'Why?'

'Because, as you said to me earlier today, I've been digging and digging and digging.' Zoltan was drawling again. But his eyes did not look lazy.

Penny took a grip on herself. 'I mean, why do you say that?'

He made an impatient noise. 'I've got eyes and ears. Because everyone else in your family thinks you're a good, cautious, quiet sort of girl who doesn't like crowds and doesn't party a lot.' His voice dropped. 'Whereas I took one look and recognised a gambler. A passionate,

reckless girl who punted everything she had and everything she was on love.'

Penny swallowed. 'No. I've changed. I'm not like that
any more.' She said slowly, 'They didn't want me to
marry Alan because they wanted me to finish my education. They said he wouldn't let me. I didn't believe
them. But they were right.'

'What happened?'

She shut her eyes, shaking her head at the weakness
of her younger self.

'I got too many prizes. It was a bad time. Alan had
a problem with a big canvas. And then someone gave
him a commission and he took so long to get started
they took it away again. Then I went and sold my stuff
in the end-of-term show. It was all too much. He—went
on a big drunk.'

'His first?'

'No.' Penny looked down at her hands. 'No, not his
first. Just—the first that I knew about. The doctors said
that I—shouldn't challenge him.'

'And?'

'And I gave up the art school.'

'And?'

'That's it. That's all.'

His eyes bored into her. It was Penny's which fell.

'No,' he said. 'That's not all. Shall we stop
pretending?' His voice was soft. 'It's perfectly clear that
your husband hurt you. You married him at nineteen.
You finally got out from the marriage—what? Five years
ago? Six? And since then you've been melting into the
background in case anyone noticed you and hurt you
again.'

Penny was perfectly white. She looked at him, her
mind a blank.

He said gently, 'I was watching you this morning when
your father was reading from the paper.'

Every muscle in her body tensed unbearably.

'He might not believe that women stay with men who hurt them physically,' Zoltan said evenly. 'But I do. If they think it's their fault. If they think they can help.' He paused. 'That's what you did, isn't it?'

There was a terrible silence. She thought, He knows it all. She could not think.

'Tell me,' he said at last, under his breath.

'Nobody has asked me that,' she said at last. '*Nobody*.'

'Then they should have done. And I'm asking now. What happened?'

She closed her eyes. 'Why do you want to know?'

He did not hesitate. 'Because I can't know you properly unless I do.'

She shook her head.

'And I need to know you properly,' Zoltan told her quietly. 'Come on, love, tell me. Then you need never think about it again. Put it behind you for ever.'

'Promises!' she said drearily. 'If I haven't got rid of it in nearly six years, it's not going to go away now.'

He didn't argue. All he did was say again, 'Tell me.'

She shrugged. 'It's fairly ordinary. Alan had a drink problem. He had had one before I met him. That summer he was down here he had been dried out. He was supposed to be starting again.'

Zoltan looked grim. But he didn't say anything. That made it easier somehow.

Penny suddenly found herself saying things she had barely even dared to remember for years.

'He was chronically jealous. Of my background, my financial security, even my place at art school. After that first almighty drunk, I was scared. The doctors wouldn't tell me anything. Except that they seemed to think I was partly responsible somehow. They treated me as if I was his enemy.' She shook her head. All the remembered bewilderment was in her eyes. 'I'd never seen anyone like that before. I was horrified. When he sobered up, he said it was my fault. I made him feel a failure.'

'You didn't go to your parents?'

'I—couldn't. They'd been against the marriage in the first place. Alan already thought they despised him.'

'Was that when he first hit you?' Zoltan asked gently.

Penny flushed. Her eyes fell. 'Yes,' she muttered.

He said something fierce under his breath. 'And no one noticed?'

'I took care that they didn't. It seemed disloyal.'

'So how did you ever get away?' He sounded angry.

'Oh, that was easy.' Penny gave a small bitter smile. 'I'd got a small commission. Alan—took a knife to my canvas. And then he came for me.'

'Hell.'

Zoltan looked bleak with shock.

'I almost expected it by then,' Penny said painfully. 'I'd even sort of half planned my exit route. I ran downstairs to neighbours. The police came and took him away. He was breaking up the flat.'

'And then?'

'Oh, then he was admitted to hospital. The specialist said that it was never going to get better as long as he was living with me. I seemed to drive him to it. He saw me as a rival, apparently, and every time I had any sort of success at all it made him doubt himself. So—I left.'

Zoltan looked at her carefully. 'How did you feel when he died?'

Penny swallowed. But she had told him so much that she was mortally ashamed of, she thought. Why hold back on this one thing?

'Free,' she said honestly.

And then she began to cry.

CHAPTER NINE

ZOLTAN let her cry. He did not attempt to touch her, although he passed across a spotless linen handkerchief at one point. When her tears showed signs of abating he got up and went to her bathroom. He came back with her tooth-mug full of water.

He hunkered down in front of her, presenting it. Penny made a little deprecating grimace, blinked, rubbed the back of her hand across her mouth and accepted the mug.

'Thank you,' she said in a rather watery voice.

He shrugged, his mouth wry. 'Least I can do.'

Penny swallowed some water. 'I don't normally behave like a waterfall.'

'I know you don't. You wouldn't have done now if I hadn't pushed you into it.' He looked at her searchingly. 'All right?' he asked softly.

She nodded, not quite meeting his eyes. He sighed and stood up.

'I wish——' he began. And stopped.

Penny blew her nose hard.

'I must look a mess.' She stole a look at him.

'No.' He looked stern and rather remote.

'Well, I'd better wash my face at least.' She inspected his handkerchief. It was no longer pristine. 'When they say mascara is waterproof they don't seem to count tears,' she said, with a gallant attempt at amusement.

'Yes, do that.' He was curt to the point where he could not have sounded less interested.

Penny flushed slightly. Well, what could she expect? she told herself. He had told her from the start that he was not into permanence. Presumably he was not into

167

floods of tears and self-pity either, no matter how temporary. What was more, she did not blame him.

She went into the bathroom and splashed cold water on her face. She inspected the results narrowly in the mirror. Her eyelids would be puffy for some hours, she thought, but at least the cold water had taken the pinkness out of them.

She blotted her cheeks carefully before reapplying make-up. Normally she did not use much. But she was not an artist for nothing, she told herself firmly. And today was hardly normal. So she went through her whole box of cosmetics, ending with artful and nearly invisible eye-shadow that made her eyes look the colour of malachite and roughly the same shape as Cleopatra's. She dragged a comb through her hair. Fortunately the expensive cut meant that the feathery tendrils fell back into place naturally.

Penny studied the resulting image in the mirror. It might not be what Zoltan Guard was used to in the glamour stakes but it was the best she could do. And Zoltan Guard was going to be on his way in a very few hours, she reminded herself. Her fingers clenched round his handkerchief in a sudden spasm of loss.

This is crazy, she told herself. I don't even like him very much. But at the thought of him going out of my life I feel lonely as I've never felt in my life before. And I've known him twenty-four hours!

Not only crazy but also embarrassing. She must not give any sign of her deplorable feelings to Zoltan, she warned herself. They might not embarrass him, of course. He was the most imperturbable man she had ever met, after all. But they would cripple her with embarrassment whenever she thought about it in the future, she knew. No, her feelings must be buried out of sight. Now.

She went back through the bedroom into her small sitting-room. She averted her eyes as she passed the bed. It was only too easy to remember him lounging there.

Was it only this morning? She winced, recalling how she had barred the door to her mother while he lay there laughing.

He was not laughing when she went into the room this time. He was looking out of the window at the sunny courtyard, an expression on his face she had not seen before. It made him look almost grim.

Penny lifted her chin.

'Sorry about that,' she said, in a voice of praise-worthy steadiness. 'I'm better now.'

He turned from the window to face her. His eyes widened slightly.

'So I see.' His look of grimness did not lessen. If any-thing it intensified. 'Do I gather that you're intending to go back to the party?'

In spite of the grimness he was still breathtakingly attractive. Penny let her eyes slide sideways. She was ter-rified he would see the hunger in them.

'I can't very well avoid it,' she pointed out reasonably. 'My sister. My home. I have to say goodbye to people.'

'Still other people first?' His voice mocked but he sounded angry. 'You could get out of it very easily. You could go and get that car of yours and we'll make a break for it.'

Her heart flared into hope for a moment. But then common sense reinstated itself. This was a man who looked for temporary satisfactions only. His affairs came with a built-in guarantee of obsolescence. Getting involved with Zoltan Guard would provide her with the second broken heart of her life. And the next one, Penny thought, would be terminal.

'I don't think that's a very good idea,' she said gently after a pause.

Zoltan looked at her moodily. 'No, I suppose not.'

She managed a smile. 'I'm grateful, though.'

The heavy brows twitched together. 'For making you cry like a waterfall?' he asked, with bitter self-mockery.

Her throat ached. But she kept her smile in place somehow.

'You were right. It had to be done some time. I've suppressed it for too long. I'm glad to have told someone. I am truly.'

'Then I'm glad to have been of service.'

But he didn't sound it. He sounded savage, Penny thought.

'I really must go back,' she said. 'Will you come too?'

He shrugged. 'Why not?'

They walked across the courtyard in uncomfortable silence. At least, Penny found it uncomfortable. Zoltan was lost in a brown study and gave every appearance of being unaware of her or anything uncomfortable in their situation.

The party was beginning to break up. As soon as Penny set foot in the front hall, Leslie pounced on her.

'There you are, Pen. You must come and say goodbye to Aunt Catherine.' She smiled briefly at Zoltan. 'Forgive me, Professor. You can have Penny back when she's done her duty.'

The heavy brows twitched together in a black line over the imperial nose. He did not smile.

'But her duty seems neverending,' Zoltan said, before turning on his heel and walking deliberately into another room.

Leslie stared after him, her mouth open.

'Good grief,' she said, awed. 'He wants to take you away from all this. Lucky girl.'

Penny's laugh broke in the middle. 'You don't know how wrong you are.'

Leslie was wearing a small private smile. 'Am I?'

Penny remembered how she had thought there was a conspiracy to matchmake when she had first seen Zoltan. If she had seen Leslie looking like this then, she would have been certain of it. And she would have been as wrong as she could be. Nobody made matches for Zoltan. Not even himself.

She shook her head. 'Completely,' she said firmly. 'The man is heart-whole. And likes his affairs to stay temporary.'

'You seem to know a lot about a man you only met yesterday.'

Penny snorted. 'Considering we spent the evening chasing burglars together——' She broke off, looking conscience-stricken.

'I know,' Leslie said peacefully.

Penny was startled.

'Zoltan mentioned it,' she said. 'He thought you were wrong keeping it from Laura. So do I, frankly. You could have done with a bit of cosseting today. After all, you're probably in shock.'

Penny thought about the way she had twined about Zoltan last night, when she had undoubtedly been in shock. And again today when she almost certainly hadn't. At least until after he touched her.

'Yes, I was probably looking for some cosseting,' she said drily. 'But I'm not going to get it and I don't waste my time chasing dreams. Take me to Aunt Catherine.'

Leslie laughed. 'One day the dreams will come looking for you,' she prophesied. 'Aunt Catherine's over there.' She nodded in the direction of the study. 'I've got to see a man about transport out of here.'

She whisked off. Penny went in search of her aunt.

Aunt Catherine had installed herself in a high-backed armchair and was holding court.

'There you are,' she greeted Penny. 'Torn yourself away from your young man for a minute?'

Penny flushed slightly. 'No young man, Aunt Catherine,' she said, bending to kiss the wrinkled cheek.

Her aunt looked at her shrewdly. 'So why have you put on eyeshadow for the first time in years? Looks good,' she added fairly.

Penny laughed at her. 'Thank you. But it's for me. Not for any mythical man.'

Aunt Catherine snorted. 'Looked a pretty substantial myth to me. Handsome devil. Difficult to manage, though, I'd have said.'

Penny looked at her in horror. Manage Zoltan? 'I wouldn't even try.'

Her aunt looked amused. 'That's strong feeling. For a myth.'

Penny felt that family affection and the respect due to age had been tried high enough. 'You're a nosy, interfering old woman and it's nothing to do with you,' she told her aunt roundly.

She looked rather pleased. 'You're right, of course. But I'd like to see you happy. And you haven't been.'

Penny was shaken. Her aunt patted her on her arm.

'Go for him,' she advised. 'If he's the one you want then don't let him walk away without telling him.' For a moment the sharp old face looked younger, sadder. 'I did. Never ceased to regret it.'

Her niece was touched—and taken aback. 'I didn't know.'

'Well, now you do. Learn by my mistakes, my girl.'

Penny bit her lip. 'But what if he doesn't want me?'

'From what I've seen,' said Aunt Catherine, looking a great deal less vulnerable, 'he wants you all right. And even if he doesn't, what have you got to lose?'

'My dignity,' protested Penny, wincing at the thought.

'Pride,' said Aunt Catherine dismissively. 'That's all it is. Pride won't keep you warm at night. And I can tell you, it's not much of a consolation either, if you're going to spend your life trying not to think what might have been.'

She hauled herself heavily to her feet and stood up, leaning on her stick. Penny took her arm. Aunt Catherine's face softened.

'You're a good, loving girl. Your marriage was a bad business but it's time you put it behind you.' She touched Penny's hand briefly. 'If you want that handsome devil with the blue eyes, tell him. Chances don't come round twice.'

Penny said, 'I'll remember that.'

'Do it,' her aunt said briskly. 'And now you can see me to my car.'

Penny did. When the driver had tucked the rug round his passenger's knees and driven off at the funeral pace Aunt Catherine demanded, she went slowly back into the house. She had to admit it, a lot of what Aunt Catherine said had echoed her own half-subconscious feelings.

She looked for Zoltan in the house. But he was nowhere to be seen. And she wasn't going to ask, she thought wryly. Leslie's teasing had been quite enough for one day. She wasn't going to give the whole family cause to eye her in the same speculative way.

There was pride and pride, she reasoned. She might—just might—sink it for Zoltan if she was feeling brave enough. But there was no way she was going to expose herself to the cheerful witticisms of her family.

The party had sunk to a desultory state. She saw Leslie, who made a face.

'Everyone is waiting for someone else to move,' she said. 'They know they all need to go off and change before the dance but no one has the energy to start.'

Penny looked at her watch. It was later than she had thought.

'What about Celia and Mike? Can't they start the exodus?'

Leslie cast her eyes to the ceiling. 'Where have you been this last couple of hours? Or perhaps I shouldn't ask.' She had her look of secret amusement again. 'They pushed off ages ago. Celia went up and changed and came down in some amazingly expensive going-away suit and they drove off into the village. Just as if,' she added acidly, 'they really were going away instead of coming back this evening for the dance. No doubt Mummy stage-managed it.'

Penny laughed. 'She wanted everything proper after the disasters the rest of us provided, I suppose.'

Leslie nodded. 'And Celia's too happy to care.' She looked at Penny narrowly. 'What about you, Pen?'

'Me? I'm ecstatic,' said Penny lightly.

'You look it,' agreed her sister drily. 'No, I meant what about the dance. What are you wearing? Do you need a ride?'

Penny stared. 'I'm not the bride. I don't need to make a ceremonial exit.'

Leslie sighed. 'I meant, do you need a ride out? The dance will go on all night, you know. And nobody in the house will get a wink of sleep. I know several people who are pushing off early. I just wondered if you'd like a lift back to town with one of them.'

'I hadn't thought,' Penny said slowly. 'Wouldn't Mummy mind?'

'Probably—if she knew. Who's going to tell her?'

Penny succumbed. 'It would be heaven.' A thought struck her. 'But I've got my car here. Damn. I suppose I could drive myself,' she said doubtfully.

Leslie looked faintly annoyed. 'Don't even think about it. You'll be much too tired, after last night's drama and all. I'll get someone to drive your car up tomorrow.'

'*Would* you?'

Leslie gave her an affectionate smile. 'Leave it with me. You deserve a break.'

Penny was touched. She was also enormously grateful.

She was even more grateful at midnight when Leslie came and touched her on the arm.

Penny had originally agreed to go to the dance out of family solidarity. She had never expected to enjoy it. For the critical hour while she was getting dressed in her new long gown she had thought that she might, after all, have fun. If Zoltan was there. If he danced with her. If they talked . . .

'I'm palpitating like a schoolgirl,' Penny told her reflection. 'This is ridiculous.'

But she couldn't stop the slight, sweet tremor of her body at the prospect.

The tremor was rapidly calmed. Registering arrival after arrival in the marquee, Penny slowly realised that Zoltan was not going to show up. She debated. She could not remark on his absence to her sisters without causing more comment than she could handle. But her new brother-in-law was a different matter.

Cautiously she remarked to Mike that his old teacher was taking a long time to get to the dance floor from his room under the eaves.

'Oh, Zoltan's gone,' Mike said.

He dragged her on to the dance floor and began to windmill his arms energetically.

'Gone?' Penny was blank. She began to dance on autopilot. 'He didn't say he was leaving.'

'He rang his secretary in Cambridge and she had some message for him,' Mike said without interest. 'He's always been like that. On the move all over the world at the drop of a hat.'

'Oh,' said Penny. After a pause she said carefully, 'Do you know where he is this time?'

'Haven't a clue,' said Mike cheerfully. 'Has he left something behind?'

'Not as far as I know.'

'Then there's no problem, is there?'

'No,' said Penny hollowly.

After that the sparkle went out of the evening. So she was relieved when Leslie tapped her on the arm.

'Get your coat,' her sister said briskly. 'Your chauffeur's leaving in ten minutes. Big dark car under the copper beech.'

'Thanks,' said Penny.

Leslie hugged her suddenly. 'Good luck.'

Surprised and moved, Penny hugged her back. 'Weddings seem to make everyone soggy,' she said, her eyes filling. 'You're a love.'

'Yes, I am. Hang on, Mummy's looking this way. I'll put up the smokescreen while you get your toothbrush.'

Penny nodded, retreating to the tented door.

'And don't forget to give me a ring,' Leslie hissed after her. 'I want to know if you get home safely.'

It was only later that Penny realised how oddly that explanation had been phrased.

CHAPTER TEN

BUT at the time Penny just darted back to her room and picked up her overnight case. She swung her frilled woollen serape round her bare shoulders against the chill of the summer evening. The edge of it caught something on the window ledge. It fell to the floor. Stooping, Penny picked it up.

It was the handkerchief Zoltan had given her. Crumpled and more than a little grubby now, it made her heart lurch. Her fingers closed round it convulsively.

'Has he left something behind?' Mike had asked.

Well, he had, hadn't he?

Here, if she wanted it, was the perfect excuse to get in touch with him again. Penny bit her lip. Did she want it?

She looked down at the scrap of crumpled linen. Oh, she did, she did. But was she brave enough to risk hurt again? 'Chances don't come round twice,' Aunt Catherine had said. She didn't want to spend the rest of her life wondering what would have happened if she had been brave enough, she realised suddenly. She stuffed the handkerchief in her pocket and tumbled downstairs.

Dropping her overnight case at the bottom, she sprinted back to the marquee. She scanned the crowd for Mike and soon located him. He had discarded his dinner jacket and was partying with enthusiasm.

'Mike,' she said, attracting his attention by the simple expedient of grabbing a handful of the back of his white shirt and pulling him backwards.

'Good lord, Pen, you going?'

'Never mind that. Where can I get hold of Zoltan Guard?'

177

He grinned. 'Old magic still working?' he asked admiringly. 'Don't know how the man does it.'

Penny ignored that. 'His address in Cambridge. Or better still a phone number.'

Mike shook his head. 'And I thought you were a sensible girl,' he mourned.

'We all lose our senses sometimes,' Penny said drily. 'Come on Mike. Give.'

'Huntingdon College,' he said. 'Don't remember the number. It's in the book. They'll know where to find him. He has rooms there.'

'Thank you,' said Penny. On impulse she kissed his cheek.

He looked pleased. 'Be careful,' he warned.

'Too late for that.' Penny suddenly found she felt inordinately cheerful. 'I'll let you know what happens.'

He shuddered. 'Cilly will kill me.'

Penny laughed and danced out into the night.

Her bag was undisturbed. She hooked it on to her shoulder and went in search of the car under the copper beech.

She wondered idly whom Leslie had instructed to drive her home. There were plenty of older couples who would be looking for their beds before dawn, she thought. She just hoped it wasn't going to be anyone who wanted to engage her in conversation all the way to London. She had too much thinking to do to make small talk.

It was, as Leslie had said, a big dark car. Penny did not know much about cars, but the sleek lines of this one were the height of expensive style. Good old Leslie, she thought with a private grin.

It was empty. Penny looked round, from the house to the marquee, wondering where her companions were coming from, when a hand came out of the darkness and unhooked the bag from her shoulder.

'You won't want that,' said a voice she knew.

Penny went absolutely still. For a moment she did not dare to turn round in case it was a fantasy.

'But you've left,' she croaked.

'I came back.'

'But—did you leave something behind?'

'Yes,' said Zoltan Guard with a soft laugh.

Penny began to tremble. She turned round. He was a tall shadow. She could not see his eyes. But somehow, through her whole body, veins and nerves and muscles, she could feel his laughter. And a fierce determination.

'What is it? I'll get it for you. Tell me where to look...' She was babbling and she knew it.

'Get in the car,' he said quietly.

'But I'll get it for you.'

There was that deep, achingly familiar note of amusement in his voice. 'You have.'

For a wild moment she thought he could see his handkerchief, scrunched up in her pocket. Then common sense reasserted itself. She blushed in the darkness.

'I don't understand,' said Penny untruthfully.

'Yes, you do.' He took her face between his hands and feathered the lightest of kisses against her mouth. 'You damned well do,' he said under his breath. 'And I'm going to prove it to you.'

A crazy happiness seemed to burst over her heart. At the same time a little forlorn wistfulness touched the moment.

'Quite temporarily,' she muttered.

'What?'

He raised his head and looked searchingly down at her in the darkness. From the marquee there came a burst of raucous laughter, then a surge of music, renewed at double amplification. It had the effect of isolating them in their corner of stillness under the copper beech.

'We'd better be moving,' Zoltan said. 'That doesn't sound like a party that's going to stay indoors for long.'

'Yes,' said Penny. She knew that she was agreeing to more than a car ride. It filled her with a reckless joy. 'Let's go.'

He tossed her bag on the capacious back seat. Then he helped her into the passenger seat, tucking her satin skirts around her, and closed the door on her. He swung into the driving seat and turned on the engine.

'We've got a lot to talk about,' he said. 'But not in imminent danger of being jumped by too many of my old students.'

He let the clutch in and the car moved forward with a luxurious purr. He looked sideways at her.

'I gather Ian has already maligned me,' he said casually.

Penny looked down at her hands, locked nervously in her lap. Why am I nervous? she thought, I've decided to do this.

She said coolly, 'He filled me in on your previous history with ladies.'

'I was afraid of that.' For once Zoltan didn't sound amused. Or very sure of himself, she noted with amazement. 'Did he tell you I was the greatest rake since Casanova?'

'Something along those lines.'

'It's not true,' he said urgently.

'It sounded awfully credible.'

He sent her another look. 'You're laughing at me,' he said on a note of discovery.

She shook her head. 'Maybe at both of us.'

'Why?'

'Well, I've steered clear of involvement since my marriage ended. It's completely out of character for me to be driving off at midnight with the greatest rake since Casanova, bound for God knows where. Or are you,' she added, injecting a faintly curious note into her voice, 'going to take me back to my flat as negotiated?'

'I'll take you wherever you want.' His voice was warm.

'You mean, it's my decision?'

'Of course.'

'Oh,' said Penny.

'You don't want it to be your decision?' He sounded bemused.

'Casanova had many faults. Or so I'm told. The great thing about his technique, though,' said Penny carefully, 'was that he swept a girl off her feet.'

'Ah. You want to be swept off your feet.' He sent her a quick look. 'Fine. I can arrange that.'

'I thought,' said Penny, with something of a snap, 'that you *had* arranged it. And that this was it.'

He reached out and brushed the back of his fingers down her cheek.

'Sweetheart, I haven't even started.'

He was driving through the lanes as if he had known them—and the car—all his life.

Penny said, 'Aren't we going a little fast?'

Zoltan chuckled. 'Faster than I've ever gone before.'

Penny did not pretend to misunderstand him. 'Is that wise?'

'Probably not.' He didn't sound worried.

Aunt Catherine, Penny thought with a sudden giggle, would approve.

'What are you laughing at?'

'Something one of my aunts said to me this evening.' She looked at him under her lashes. 'She told me not to let you get away, if I wanted you.'

'I'll second that.'

She was slightly put out. 'Yes, but do I?' she said captiously.

He turned the car on to the big dual carriageway. In the sudden light of the overhead streetlamps he looked deceptively serious, she thought.

'It's up to me to see you do.'

He didn't say much for the next hour. He was obviously concentrating on directions. Penny, to whom the road was unfamiliar, did not offer to help. Well, at least he wasn't taking her back to London, she thought, pleased.

'Where did you get the car?' she asked at one point, as they hit a motorway and he put his foot down. 'I didn't think they rented out cars of this quality in case they got beaten up.'

The car glided smoothly into hyperspeed. The engine noise stayed at the same drowsy purr. Zoltan shrugged.

'It's mine. I'm over here so much I keep a car in the UK.'

Penny sat up. 'Then why did I have to meet you at the station?' she demanded, put out.

'A friend had borrowed it. I had someone drive it over to Shrewsbury for me. I picked it up this afternoon.'

'Oh,' said Penny, digesting this. She snuggled down again in luxury upholstery.

Luxury cars that he used less than half the year. A car delivery service to all corners of the country. It added up to an unnervingly expensive lifestyle. She had realised he was not a hungry academic. But this?

'Are you terribly rich?' she said with foreboding.

Zoltan laughed. 'I pay my bills and I buy the toys I want. Like the car. I can earn as much as I want. I choose my own jobs. Apart from that, I'm a free man.'

Penny digested that.

'I don't understand,' she said mischievously, looking at him from under her lashes.

He reached out and squeezed her fingers hard. It made her catch her breath in a sudden flash-flood of desire. From the taut look on his face, it had the same effect on him.

'Does it matter how much money I have?' he said, sounding strangled.

Penny hesitated. 'I don't think I'd like to be a millionaire's mistress,' she said at last in a small voice. 'I'm sorry but——'

'*What*?'

'I dare say it seems very silly to you but——'

'We are not,' said Zoltan grimly, 'talking about mistresses.'

'Oh,' said Penny again, in an entirely different voice.

'I'm not talking about it in the car,' he told her hastily. 'You're a severe enough trial to my blood-pressure as it is.'

'Oh,' said Penny, pleased. 'No one has ever told me I'm a trial to their blood-pressure before.'

'You probably just didn't understand them,' Zoltan said maliciously. He reached out a long arm and tucked the woollen wrap more securely round her. 'Or they hadn't sat next to you for hours while your damned shawl slid off your bare shoulders. It's extremely disquieting.'

Penny blushed deeply. 'Good,' she said.

'I'm glad you think so. I am seriously considering confiscating that dress permanently when we arrive.'

'Arrive where?' she asked, to cover her confusion.

'My house in Cambridge. Since you expressed a desire to be swept off your feet, that's the best I can do at a moment's notice.' He touched her face again, as if he wanted to keep assuring himself that she was actually in the car beside him. 'Tomorrow any South Sea paradise you care to name.'

Penny choked. 'Don't be ridiculous. I've got a job.'

'I know. It's extremely inconvenient. But I have given it some thought and I think I've got the answer. Surely even hospital administrators are allowed time off for honeymoons?'

Penny went very still. All of a sudden all desire to laugh left her.

'Honeymoons?'

'Well, I was only thinking of one,' Zoltan told her amused. 'With me.'

'You did say honeymoon?' Penny said gropingly. 'As in legal matrimony?'

'That's the one.'

'But—you don't believe in permanence.'

'Twenty-four hours ago,' Zoltan said superbly, 'I didn't believe in love at first sight either. We can all learn from our mistakes.'

Penny drew a sharp breath.

'Can't we?' he asked softly.

She bit her lip. 'I don't know,' she said honestly. 'I seem to have made so many.'

'I can only think of one.'

He turned the car off the big road and swung it round a succession of roundabouts. A shadowed signpost said Cambridge. Penny's hands clenched tight in her lap.

'No, make that two,' he added in a thoughtful voice.

They were travelling down a tree-lined street with big gothic villas on either side, set back amid gardens like woodland groves. Without warning Zoltan turned the car in under a laburnum tree. The catkins were gold in the headlights for a moment. Then they died as he cut the engine and the lights.

Into the silence Penny said in an unnaturally bright voice, 'Only two?'

'Yup. One, when you married Alan Dane in the first place.'

He reached back and hefted her overnight bag from the back seat. He leaned in front of her and opened her door for her. He kissed her briefly.

'And two, not going to bed with me last night.'

Penny swallowed deafeningly in the silence of the car. She couldn't think of a thing to say.

'Never mind,' he told her forgivingly. 'We're going to put that right now.'

He took her into the house with one arm round her shoulders, as if he was afraid to let her go. It was a tall house with winding stairs and odd corners, full of pictures and books. Not unlike her own flat, Penny thought, startled, although he obviously had more money to spend. But the feeling of favourite things and untidy comfort was the same.

Perhaps it was for that reason that she suddenly clutched the serape tight around her. She found herself hoping desperately that Zoltan was not going to stampede her up to bed at once. She felt too strange in this familiar and yet not familiar house. He sensed her unease.

'Come into the study and warm up,' he said softly.

He did not take his arm from around her shoulders. Penny began to feel the tension easing. She even leaned her head briefly against his shoulder as he pushed open a doorway off the hall.

'I work in here,' he said, gesturing with the other hand. 'To prove it, to the left you will see my collected works.'

Penny gasped. She saw at once where he was pointing. For there, along the oak shelves, were two lines of them. Thin books, tall books, immensely fat books. In every language she could think of and some she couldn't. All of them saying on their spines 'Zoltan Guard'. It was oddly intimidating. Penny looked at him with astonishment—and reluctant awe. She suddenly felt horribly out of her depth.

But she said as lightly as she could manage, 'I see what you mean, Professor.'

The arm round her tightened.

'Don't look like that,' he said irritably. 'I told you—I do what I'm interested in. I have a lot of energy, there aren't many people in my field, so I get a lot of work. It's chance. Being a professor is largely chance too.'

Penny stared round the room. It was a large room and apart from his own works books filled all the wall space that wasn't taken up by windows or the fireplace. There were more books and papers on a battered oak desk.

'That's not what it looks like,' she said wryly.

'Don't be taken in by Dracula's Castle Library,' he said. 'It comes with the job description. That's what it means to be a professor. By the time you get to professor you've done the subject to death.'

There was a slight hint of defensiveness in his voice. Penny considered the handsome face above her and reached a conclusion.

'Are you embarrassed about all these books?' she demanded.

She could feel his heart beating under her shoulderblade.

'They must look stuffy to a gorgeous creature like you.'

Penny turned in his arms and looked up into his face.

'Are you joking?' she said incredulously.

He looked down at her, the blue eyes for once uncertain.

'Not stuffy?'

'The greatest rake since Casanova,' Penny told him firmly, 'is not stuffy.' When he did not seem reassured, she reached up and kissed his chin. 'You promised you'd warm me up.'

'Oh.' He looked disconcerted. 'Yes, of course. It's chilly in here. I'll light the fire.'

'I was not,' said Penny, blushing furiously but keeping her head high and her voice conversational, 'thinking of a fire. Or of staying in here either.'

He didn't seem to be able to speak. He seemed to have turned to stone. It was clearly going to be up to her to make matters progress, Penny realised.

Ignoring her heated cheeks, she went on bravely, 'To be honest, I was rather hoping you'd take me to bed.'

His arms went round her convulsively. They tightened like a vice, knocking the breath out of her.

'Oh, my darling,' said Zoltan, shaken.

They kissed long and passionately. At last he released her. Penny's head swam. Her serape had fallen to the rug where it spilled over a pile of books and papers. So great was the oxygen deprivation, she thought, amused, that she felt the world swaying round her.

And then she realised that it really was swaying. Zoltan had put one hand behind her knees, the other like a bar across her shoulders, and swung her up to lie across his chest.

'This is ridiculous,' gasped Penny, hanging on to him in alarm.

He laughed down at her, the blue eyes dancing.

'You wanted to be swept off your feet. Here we go.'

His bedroom was right at the top of the house. By the time they reached it they were both helpless with laughter. Still holding her, Zoltan collapsed on the bed.

'The lady's fantasies fulfilled,' he said smugly.

Penny struggled up on one elbow. 'No, they jolly well aren't. You've got a lot more to do before you can start putting that in your autobiography.'

His eyes glinted down at her. 'It will,' he said softly, 'be my pleasure.' His mouth tilted in a smile that was entirely wicked. 'But first of all I'm confiscating that damned provocative dress as a matter of public safety.'

He began to kiss her, laughing. Then, as their clothes fell, and the first fingers of light signalled the dawn, they laughed no more.

Later Penny lay in his arms, dazed into silence. Zoltan, she had found, made love with an intensity of concentration that made her feel like the most precious creature in the whole world. He had brought her exquisitely alive in every atom of her being and then had taken that being to heights of quivering sensation she had not even imagined could be possible.

And then he had told her that he loved her.

'Oh, darling,' said Penny, overwhelmed.

He looked down at her, absorbedly combing her hair round the curve of her neck.

'It's never happened before. I didn't really think it could,' he confessed. 'I thought that only not very bright people fell in love.'

Penny gave a choke of laughter. He looked reproachful.

'I know. I know. But I thought I knew so much about the human condition, human feelings. And I knew all about my own. I've been trained to analyse all my life, after all. I just didn't think there was room for people to feel like this.'

He kissed her. Penny kissed him back.

'And now that you do?'

'I'd like to get married,' he said soberly. 'I told you in the car. I—know you may have reservations. But not all the men in the world are like Alan. I'm sure given time...'

He stopped. Penny had bounced into a sitting position.

'Are you saying you thought I wouldn't marry you?' she demanded. 'That I was the one with objections to marriage, I mean.'

'Well, yes. You said—this afternoon——'

'Yesterday afternoon,' Penny corrected.

'All right, pedant. Yesterday afternoon. You said it wasn't a very good idea.'

Penny drew a deep calming breath. Otherwise she would have screamed.

'But that was because I thought you were going to love and leave me, you stupid man,' she said in exasperation.

Zoltan looked blank. 'What?'

'That was your reputation,' she pointed out. 'And it was you yourself who told me you weren't into permanence. What would you have thought in my place?'

'Exactly what you did,' he admitted after a moment.

'And I spent a miserable afternoon wishing that I'd been braver. And then I found the hankie you'd lent me when I was crying and I thought, That's all the excuse I need. I'll follow him to the ends of the earth and see if he'll give me another chance.'

Zoltan stared into her eyes, fascinated. '*Did* you?'

'Yes, I did. I was going to sink my pride completely for you. And you don't seem to appreciate it at all,' Penny said, glaring.

He reached up for her and pulled her down to him firmly.

'I do. I do. I'm luckier than I deserve and I'm never going to let you go. I didn't realise. My darling, you are quite right; I'm a stupid man.'

Penny sighed and wriggled against him, pulling the covers over both of them again.

'No, you aren't,' she said blissfully. 'You're wonderful. You just don't notice when people are madly in love with you. I'm going to marry you and make sure you never make the same mistake again.'

He gathered her against his chest. She could feel the rumble of laughter as he sought her mouth.

'I rely on that,' he said.

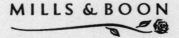

SLOW BURN
Heather Graham Pozzessere

Faced with the brutal murder of her
husband, Spencer Huntington demands
answers from the one man who should have
them—David Delgado—ex-cop, her
husband's former partner and best
friend…and her former lover.

Bound by a reluctant partnership, Spencer
and David find their loyalties tested by
desires they can't deny. Their search for the
truth takes them from the glittering world of
Miami high society to the dark and
dangerous underbelly of the city—while
around them swirl the tortured secrets and
desperate schemes of a killer driven to
commit his final act of violence.

"Suspenseful…Sensual…Captivating…"

Romantic Times (USA)

MIRA

Paperback Writer...

Have you got what it takes?

For anyone who has ever thought about writing a **Mills & Boon** Romance, but just wasn't sure where to start, help is at hand...

As a result of ever increasing interest from budding authors, **Mills & Boon** have compiled a cassette and booklet package which explains in detail how to set about writing a romantic novel and answers the most frequently posed questions.

The cassette and booklet contain valuable hints that can be applied to almost any form of creative writing.

There isn't an easy recipe for writing a romance, but our cassette and booklet will help point you in the right direction—just add imagination to create your own success story!